SKYSTONE CANYON

DIANE J. REED

Cover design by Najla Qamber at Najla Qamber Designs,
www.najlaqamberdesigns.com

꽃 I 꽃

"You gotta be kidding me!" argued Barrett Iron Feather. "You want me to patrol a movie set, when I got leads on busting Tricky Jake's meth ring? I've been working on this case for weeks! Do you hear me? Weeks!" He slammed his department-issue mobile phone several times on the dash.

"Barrett…Barrett! Anger management! Deep breaths…try to control your rage, like they taught you in class. Are you listening to me?" replied the police chief on the other end of the line.

After a few more whacks to the phone for good measure, Barrett rolled his eyes and ignored the police chief's ongoing chatter. He leaned back in his cruiser that was parked in a turn-out by the side of a twisty mountain road, scanning the view of snow-capped peaks in the faint hope of harnessing his temper.

It didn't work—

He hammered the phone a couple of more times on the dash.

Shaking his head, Barrett returned the dented device to his ear. "I don't care what the hell you say," he spit out in a defiant tone. "There's not a goddamn thing you can do to convince me to do sissy work, babysitting a bunch of pampered city slickers from LA when I could be ridding the streets of vermin like Tricky Jake—"

"First of all," the police chief cut him off, "Jake got dragged to jail this morning for a DUI and driving with a suspended license. I know it's not much, but it will keep him out of trouble for a while till we can reschedule your sting. And second of all, short of the last gold rush over a hundred years ago, this movie's the best thing to happen to the town of Bandits Hollow. Nell Granger is putting up the film crew at her Golden Wagon Hotel for a pretty price and catering the entire enterprise from her restaurant. She's been practically a mother to you, Barrett—think what this will do for her business. And Mayor Dirk Meriwether's been selling authentic western wear like hotcakes to the costume department from his mercantile. Then there's the tourism exposure the town will get for being featured in a film on Wings, the popular movie channel. To be clear, Officer Iron Feather, I'm not asking you, *I'm ordering you* to serve as head of security for the *Skystone Canyon* movie set. If any of the actors or extras get injured, it could blow this whole deal for Bandits Hollow—and we desperately need the revenue."

"This is political bullshit, isn't it?" Barrett accused in a rough tone. "If you weren't best friends with the mayor, he wouldn't be hitting you up for free security for some stupid film. Paid for by taxpayers, I might add."

"God, you're a cynical," the police chief sighed. "You know perfectly well I've been offered bribes by underworld players for years and never taken a dime. I believe in this town, Barrett, and I want what's good for it. So get your ass home and change into your rodeo gear and ride that trusty roping horse of yours—the one that's focused as hell and bombproof in crowds—over to Bandits Hollow right now."

"Wait, I gotta dress like I'm *in* the movie? On my *horse?*" Barrett replied, flabbergasted. "What's next, makeup and fricking hairspray?"

"The western attire is stipulated in the contract by the Wings Channel. They want everyone near the set to be wearing period garb so when cameras sweep over the town, nothing will look out of place. Including security—which is why you need your horse."

Barrett dropped his forehead with a thud on the steering wheel in disbelief. "So you're saying I have to do rhinestone cowboy patrol for a movie now? You know I'll never hear the end of it from my brothers Dillon and Lander. Am I getting paid extra for this?"

"I feel your pain—I really do," replied the police chief. "So I'll pay you regular during your shift and time and a half on your days off to work till filming ends, which is about two weeks. In the meantime, all you gotta do is sit on your horse and watch out for people's safety. Oh, and free meals from the Golden Wagon Restaurant. Not a bad gig, Barrett."

"Then why the hell can't Kevin do it? He weighs nearly a

hundred pounds more than me and loves sitting on his ass and eating Nell's food."

"Because Kevin's got a stomach bug and is throwing up in the station as we speak."

The police chief turned his phone on speaker mode so Barrett could hear the undeniable lurching sounds of his colleague vomiting in the station bathroom.

"Damn," Barrett groaned. "Of all the luck. Tell Kevin I hope he feels better. He owes me big time."

"Copy that," the police chief said. "And Barrett," he sighed, "as much as I hate to admit it, you're the best damn officer I've ever seen in all my years in law enforcement. Heaven knows, you've always had my back, and you saved my ass six months ago in that shootout when we apprehended Fitz's gang. But can you please do me a favor?"

"I don't owe you any favors."

"Then promise me one thing. Out of human decency, for Christ's sake."

"I'm not decent, either."

"Cut it out, Barrett," the police chief's voice became testy. "Just don't get into a fist fight with anybody—no matter how bad of an asshole he is. Especially one of those Hollywood types, okay?"

Barrett fell silent for a long pause. His free hand clenched into ball.

"At this point, Chief," he finally replied, "I ain't promising a goddamned thing. If you want to keep the peace, you'd better start praying right now that none of those Hollywood cowboy wannabes are idiots. Because it ain't my job to fix stupid."

2

"*Skystone Canyon* crew!" blared a man with a megaphone decked out in a tangerine rodeo shirt and tight jeans with stoplight-red cowboy boots that came up to his knees. "Filming to resume in thirty minutes!"

Barrett shook his head, wondering if the gaudy director in his pimped-out cowboy duds had ever *seen* a cow before. It wasn't hard for Barrett to blend into this period western film while he diligently rode guard on his buckskin Sand, a tall horse with a feather cattle brand on his hindquarters from the Iron Feather brothers' ranching enterprise. Barrett's chaps, boots, and hundred-year-old saddle all bore scuff marks of authenticity from helping his brother Lander run cattle for the last five years, along with winning scores of belt buckles in roping events. What was new, however, was seeing the fleet of Hollywood cameras and lighting equipment parked at the edge of Bandits Hollow. They were stationed to capture scenes of this film about a pioneer widow who keeps her ranch despite all the odds, only to find love with a handsome cowboy drifter. On this particular afternoon, Barrett's job was to keep the free-range Herefords away from the film crew and extras, should any be inclined to charge.

Luckily, one thing Barrett knew was cattle.

It was typical for him in his police work to be hyper-vigilant, detecting the slightest glance or hand movement that might indicate a criminal was about to pull a gun. And he'd known since childhood that horses telegraph everything—it was never a secret from the angry laying down of ears or brisk swishes of tails when they were about to kick, bite, or buck. But when it came to cattle, Barrett found himself actually feeling sorry for the film crew from LA. Even the stupidest stare from a bull or a cow with a newborn calf could mean he or she was about to charge—fully prepared to gore anyone or anything in sight.

For this reason, Barrett kept his eye on a white-faced cow with her young calf nearby. At any moment, she might raise her head and give him one of those fixed looks with her tail out of joint and her hooves riveted to the ground, meaning not that she'd turned to stone, but rather, that she intended to mow down the crew in a matter of seconds. As Barrett surveyed the actors and extras milling around, it was clear none of them had a clue that this thousand-pound animal could plow into them and create total mayhem before they even realized what happened.

So maybe the police chief was right, Barrett grumbled to himself. Security for a passel of pretend cowboys who've never been around livestock was probably a smart idea.

And the truth was, the Herefords were extras in *Skystone Canyon*, just like the historic town of Bandits Hollow. The cattle served as a bucolic backdrop to give the movie the feel of the old West, which was why the Wings Channel had chosen this location in Colorado with its towering mountains and picturesque meadows that reached 9,000-feet in elevation. The landscape was breathtaking by anyone's measure, and the wooden boardwalks and Victorian architecture of the town only enhanced its western appeal. But what really caught Barrett's eye that afternoon was a young woman in a yellow calico dress who was leaning against a fence rail near where *Skystone Canyon* was filming. Though her sleeves were rolled up and her dress and boots were dusty like she'd spent all morning feeding and checking on the herd, her blue eyes lit up with a soft sparkle when she spied Barrett's buckskin horse. The way she took in the animal's coloring—a warm beige tone with a black mane and tail and a distinct dorsal stripe down his back—made the horse seem familiar to her. Carefully, she studied the contours of the animal's face and large, dark eyes, almost as though she recognized him. To Barrett's surprise, she left the fence and took several strides, then stopped to stare intently at his horse. Sweeping her long, light-brown hair with honey highlights from her face, she squinted as if she were measuring the animal's features against some cobweb of memory. Even without any sign of makeup, and more than a few seeds of hay in her hair, the woman's finely-sculpted features, apple cheeks, and determined eyebrows combined to make her look…

Beautiful.

Barrett couldn't quite explain it. Nothing about her

matched the typical Hollywood idea of "pretty". She was completely natural, her windblown hair untouched by bleach or hairspray, and her tan, lightly-freckled skin a bit crinkled at the corners of her mouth and eyes, clearly devoid of Botox. She was the polar opposite of the other actresses loitering around the set, who'd had so much plastic surgery and injectable fillers that their faces looked oddly waxy, like mannequins in broad daylight. Not to mention that their busts were artificially prominent for their skinny physiques and pressed against the fabric of their period costumes until the seams nearly burst. The young woman in the yellow dress appeared more authentic, as though she'd not long ago stepped out of a Conestoga wagon that had crossed the country on a pioneer trail. And in her stern gaze was the kind of resignation befitting the time period, as if the harsh sun and brutal elements had somehow changed her. "Pretty" seemed to be her last concern. From Barrett's experience at sizing up strangers on the spot, he concluded her focus was more about...

Survival.

Being strong.

And tough enough to handle anything that came her way.

Except for that hint of sparkle that glimmered in her eyes at the sight of Barrett's horse. Glancing around at the film crew who were finishing lunch, she took another few steps closer to the buckskin.

"S-Sand?" she said, her voice brimming with hope.

The horse's ears perked up immediately. To Barrett's astonishment, the animal took a step toward her and issued a soft nicker, tossing his head in recognition.

"It's you, isn't it?" Her lips broke into a wide smile, lighting up her whole face. In an instant, her beauty was as breathtaking as a fresh sunrise. Before Barrett knew it, the woman had thrown her arms around Sand's neck.

"My old friend!" she gasped, stroking him with tears misting in her eyes. Sand nuzzled affectionately against her shoulder, and she leaned on his neck and gave him several pats.

"Oh, how I've missed you," she whispered. "You were the only thing that summer before freshman year that felt real for me. Well, except for the boy who used to own you."

The earnest sincerity in the woman's voice blew Barrett away. In his years as a police officer, he'd become an expert on lies. Hell, he heard them a hundred times a day. But the genuineness in this woman's reaction to Sand could never be faked.

The woman sent a shy glance to Barrett in the saddle. "Hi. I, um, knew this horse once," she explained, a little embarrassed by her impulsive outburst. He noticed, however, that she kept her hand on Sand as if he were a conduit to precious memories. The woman searched Barrett's big brown eyes, his chiseled cheekbones and jaw that hinted at his half-Apache heritage, along with his short dark hair the color of midnight. "I came to this town ten years ago for horse camp."

She stared off into the distance for a moment and shrugged. "Well, fat camp, to be honest. I'd just turned fourteen." She glanced down at her healthy frame and winced. "My dad was my manager back then, and he was convinced I needed to be skinnier to land acting roles. But I met the most amazing boy my age who showed me how to ride." She thought for a second and shook her head. "No, it was more than that. He showed me how to really listen to his horse... and to my heart. That boy and Sand changed my whole life."

Adrenaline skipped through Barrett's veins at her words. Throughout all of his near-misses with death in law enforcement, he'd never felt such a raw, powerful rush surge through his system the way it did now. It was a mixture of joy and shock—like finding out that someone who'd disappeared long ago had been found safe and sound over a decade later. For a moment, all Barrett could see in his mind's eye was the way a large, brutal man had come up to his best friend that summer and slapped her so hard she'd dropped to the ground.

Barrett had proceeded to beat him to a pulp.

"Lainey? Lainey Neil?" Barrett gasped. In no time, he'd slid from his saddle to the ground and stood before her, his six-foot frame towering protectively over hers. Arms stiffened, he resisted the overwhelming urge to hug the stuffing out of her and gazed into her vibrant blue eyes. "It's me—Barrett Iron Feather."

He reached up a hand and stroked Sand's smooth neck, who was only four when the two of them had met Lainey. The horse was fourteen now and at the top of his game in competitive roping. "I'm sorry I didn't recognize you," Barrett added. He studied her features with a glint of familiarity in his eyes, recalling how Lainey had been several inches shorter that summer. Then his gaze roamed over her figure, noting the nice curves of her breasts and hips. His lips curled into a slight smile—she'd filled out in a few other places, too. "Guess we've both grown up a lot since then," he said.

"Barrett!" Lainey burst, hugging him with all her might,

despite his initial hesitation. He responded by wrapping his large arms tightly around her, feeling as though he'd stepped into a dream. For some reason, her warm body against his felt downright...magical. It was as if she'd belonged there all along, and their sudden embrace had the power to transport them both back to that younger time. To a time before his parents died in a car crash. Before those miserable years he and his brothers spent at the Wilson Ranch for Wayward Boys. Before he'd become a police officer and seen the worst humanity had to offer. To a time when he was still...

Innocent.

And from the weary resignation he'd spied in her face earlier, he figured that was a time when Lainey had felt more innocent, too.

Barrett felt the throb of Lainey's heart pounding through the thin calico of her dress. She pulled back a little, a flush rising to her cheeks. Scanning his face, a sharp recognition registered in her eyes. In that moment, Barrett realized his features had hardened, too.

As hard as steel.

Everyone in Bandits Hollow knew about the cruel treatment Barrett had endured for being a half-breed at the Wilson Ranch for Wayward Boys that had permanently scarred him and his brothers. People in town naturally assumed he'd gone into police work as a career out of his rage to bust the bad guys—the "bullies"—in order to compensate for those years of torment.

But they were wrong.

It was all because of Lainey.

She was the kindest, most beautiful girl he'd ever seen. As

an extra hand at the horse camp that summer, Barrett had been forced to watch the way her domineering father constantly browbeat her, telling her she was fat—lazy—untalented—and would never amount to anything unless she obeyed his orders. When the day came that Barrett saw him strike Lainey in the middle of a horse corral, he vowed right then and there that he'd never let another innocent creature fall victim to such a man again.

And he'd followed through on his promise with his fists until her dad was nearly unconscious.

Then Barrett had taken Lainey aside while her father was moaning on the ground and showed her the moves for how to hit back in the future. He gripped her shoulders and stared her in the eye and made her promise never to take abuse from anyone again.

With tears streaming down her cheeks, Lainey had promised.

For a moment, Barrett clenched his fists, his knuckles creased white over that old, bitter memory. In silence, he gazed at the contours of Lainey's face—the curve of her forehead, cheeks and chin, before taking in those striking blue eyes he recalled from adolescence. Yes, there were slight lines etched across her forehead that shouldn't be there for a woman who was only 24, indicating that life had been hard on her as well. But Lainey's eyes still had a certain…hope. Along with that iron determination that said she was a fighter.

No wonder she'd taken on a role as a tough pioneer woman in *Skystone Canyon*, he thought.

"Lainey Neil!" bellowed the director from his megaphone,

jolting Barrett's attention. "For crying out loud, get over here! Time to film scene four."

"I-I gotta go," Lainey stammered with apology in her voice, her arms still linked around Barrett. "I hope you enjoy, you know, the movie." A smile hinted at the corner of her lips as if she didn't really want to let go. But then she released him and inhaled a deep breath, her chest rising, as though walking toward the director was like heading into battle. Before she turned to leave, Barrett gently grasped her arm.

"Maybe we could catch up some time? At the Golden Wagon Restaurant, like we used to back in the day." He squeezed her arm and gave her a wink. "Nell's still famous for her steak platter."

"I'm afraid there's not much time for that," scolded a middle-aged woman with red curly hair, interrupting their conversation. She butted between them and thrust a cosmetic brush full of powder into Lainey's face, making her cough. "Easton says time is money," the woman sighed, "and he wants to wrap *Skystone Canyon* as fast as possible." She turned to Barrett and thrust out her hand to shake his. "Hi, I'm Deb Griffin—Lainey's makeup artist, among other things." She turned and ambushed Lainey with another pat of powder.

"Deb!" Lainey complained, hacking. "I told you I don't want *any* makeup for this film. It's not authentic for the time period."

"Smoke and mirrors, sweetie," Deb remarked in a maternal tone. "Movies are all about illusion, and we've been together on sets for a decade. When have I ever made you look unnatural?"

Lainey sighed and set her hand on Deb's shoulder. "You've got a point. You're like family to me."

"And family knows best," Deb gave her a comforting smile. "Now you'd better get over to that director, before he fires us all."

※ 3 ※

Easton Wolfe stood with his hands on his hips, his cheeks so red he appeared ready to ignite into an apoplectic fit. He stomped his cowboy boot, making dirt erupt at his heel into a cloud.

"Dammit, Lainey, you're supposed to be on your horse at your mark! I can't stand former child actresses who think the whole world revolves around them. Weren't you in that stupid *Mr. Ed* remake where the horse actually *talked?* How embarrassing—"

"*Horse Feathers*," Lainey inserted before Easton could get on a roll, her voice surprisingly banal. She glanced at a corral beyond the movie trailers, noticing that the bay mare she was supposed to ride wasn't even saddled yet. "It was the network's biggest show for six seasons," she added in a flat tone without making eye contact. From the look on her face, it appeared that any interaction with Easton simply confirmed her opinion that he was a high-maintenance jerk.

"Great, so that makes you a diva now?" Easton huffed, crossing his arms. "Well, this is a movie honey, not some cheesy TV show. Which means you'd better learn to take orders."

He marched to a patch of grass that had been spray painted with a red X. "Right here, right now. Hustle!"

"Don't I need a horse?" Lainey snapped back, annoyed that Easton was putting a rush on a scene that wasn't supposed to start for another twenty minutes. "The crew is still on lunch break."

"I don't care if they starve to death and we have to use a stick horse," Easton fumed, "when I say hit your mark, you'd better hop to it!"

Lainey didn't bother to roll her eyes at his demands, deaf to Easton's constant barrage of criticism by now. It was no secret in the industry that he treated actors like dirt, and he was known for running shoe-string productions that always finished before deadline—saving the studio tons of money. And since the Wings Channel was trying to compete in the low-budget world of wholesome, feel-good TV movies with a touch of romance, the faster they wrapped, the better. Easton could take any script and serve it up into movie form within a couple of months, keeping fresh titles churning for eager viewing audiences. It didn't matter to Easton if the characters were shallow, the romance was trite, and the films had syrupy soundtracks that required insulin to endure—as long as he was handsomely paid.

Talk about cheesy.

But at 24, Lainey Neil was already considered a has-been in Hollywood. Until out of the blue, she'd been offered the female lead in a "pioneer pulp" film—a chance to star in a predictable historical western where a lonely widow struggles to hold down her cattle spread, only to be rescued by a dashing cowboy who miraculously arrives to help her.

Ten actresses had already passed on the project, with good reason.

Pioneer pulp hardly made women stars or advanced their careers. These films existed to inflate the visibility of up-and-coming heartthrobs. The male roles were typically handed to young actors on the rise who needed to demonstrate bankable charm so they could get breaks in hotter films.

Lainey's whole job was to be plain and invisible.

A blank slate for female viewers to project themselves upon, relishing in the rescue by the fantasy cowboy of their dreams.

But Lainey didn't see it that way at all.

After poring over the script, she saw an opportunity to portray her character Ada Holdwell as an incredibly brave young woman who'd been knocked down by life and refused to give up. Who was going to define herself on her own terms and thrive, come hell or high water.

A lot like Lainey.

For her, the cowboy romantic interest was incidental—because what this script had that was missing from the other low-budget films she'd been offered was a woman with…grit. Her character could have sold out. She could have high-tailed it back to her East Coast relatives, or simply married a lonely rancher nearby who she didn't love for room, board, and protection.

But she didn't.

Ada had stuck it out and decided to stay and write her own rules—even if it meant bucking against the expectations of women for her time. This was *her* ranch now, and she was going to hang onto it, even if she died trying.

To Lainey, that made Ada the real star, regardless of whichever "hunk-of-the-moment" actor was cast to play her love interest.

Lainey gave the bedraggled film assistant a kind smile has he rushed to drag the bay mare to the red X on the grass, clearly still chewing on his sandwich from lunch.

"Thank you," Lainey whispered with a pat on his shoulder. She took the reins and checked the saddle he'd just slapped onto the mare to make sure the cinch was tight enough. Then she stepped up to the horse's muzzle and gently blew into her nostrils. The mare's ears perked up and she issued a soft puff in response.

From his position behind the cameras on his horse Sand, Barrett did a double take.

He was the one who'd taught Lainey that natural horse greeting all those years ago.

It was a fundamental gesture of equine etiquette—the way horses commonly greeted one another with respect. He watched as Lainey reached up and rubbed the mare behind her ears. The horse tilted her head and leaned into Lainey's fingers, enjoying the warm display of affection.

Barrett had taught Lainey that, too.

"Good afternoon, Cinnamon," Lainey said kindly to the

horse. Taking her time, she stroked the horse's velvety, black muzzle until she appeared relaxed. Then Lainey reached to her neck and steadily ran her hand toward the mare's withers so it was no surprise what she was about to do. She quietly moved to the horse's side and wedged her left foot in the stirrup and, with an artful jump, swung into the saddle. The horse appeared calm and ready for the ride.

Another lesson in horsemanship she'd gotten from Barrett Iron Feather.

"It's about time!" bellowed Easton from his megaphone as Lainey tightened up her reins. The horse stood to attention, waiting on the slightest nudge from her heels.

"Okay, I want you to walk the horse out to that pasture," he pointed to the green meadow, "and scan those cows like you're worried rustlers might have taken a few. Got that?"

Lainey gave him a nod. She'd read the script so many times she could have done it in her sleep.

An assistant stepped in front of the cameraman and held up the clapboard for Scene 4, Take 1 of *Skystone Canyon*. He lifted the clapstick and slammed it down, making a crisp sound for the audio check. As the digital camera began to film, Lainey urged the bay mare into a walk, looking entirely natural in the saddle as her body gently swayed to the horse's rhythm. She scanned the herd, her face as full of gravity as John Wayne's in a classic western while her eyes silently tallied her head of cattle. Then she arched a brow with a concerned look, so audiences would know in that moment that her count had come up short. Without waiting for further orders from the director, she pushed Cinnamon into a trot to get closer to the herd, when the mare suddenly kicked up her heels and threw a nasty buck. Keeping her cool, Lainey prodded the horse forward into a canter, wondering what had set her off and if a retake would be ordered. Without warning, the mare burst into a break-neck gallop as though she'd been shot from a cannon. Startled, Lainey employed all the tricks she could think of to slow Cinnamon down—wriggling the reins to make her respond to the bit, abruptly leaning her shoulders back to change her center of gravity for leverage, even pulling with all her might on one rein to force the mare into a circle to slow down.

Nothing worked—

Cinnamon's hooves drummed beneath her, racing in a fury like a bat out of hell.

When Barrett saw that the bay mare was only gaining momentum—and for some reason, the film crew couldn't start their ATVs—he suddenly realized it was up to him to handle the emergency.

Fast.

Gathering his reins, he cued Sand to rocket from a standstill to a full-blown gallop, the way they'd done for years in competitive tie-down events. The seasoned roping horse with massive hindquarters charged after Lainey and the mare, having no trouble catching up to them in seconds.

"Holy shit!" Easton cried, craning his neck. "Keep the cameras rolling! We can't afford stuntmen that good. Don't let this footage go to waste." He turned to a cameraman. "Make sure the guy's face is out of the picture so we can use it in the final cut."

The film crew watched in amazement as Barrett easily rode up alongside the bay mare and slipped his arm around

Lainey's waist, scooping her into the front of his saddle faster than they could say "trick rider". His horse Sand never flinched. The moment Lainey landed in front of Barrett, her mare slowed and began to buck in place as though her tail were on fire. Barrett brought Sand to a halt and jumped down, leaving Lainey with the reins. He boldly walked up to the mare that was crow-hopping in a rage and seized her by the bridle. The film crew could tell from a distance he was talking to her in a soothing tone, which appeared to make her settle down. Cinnamon continued to dance in place for a while, when Barrett slid his hand along her neck and gave her a reassuring pat to indicate she'd done nothing wrong. With lightning speed, he unraveled the leather strap from her cinch and whipped off the saddle, setting it on the ground. The mare heaved a breath as if she'd been released from a bad spell. A moment later, she tucked her head against Barrett's shoulder as if to say thank you.

Easton turned to the rest of the crew. "Well whaddya know, we've got some kind of horse magician among us. Isn't that the police guy contracted for security?" He shot a glance at a handsome young actor with disheveled dark hair seated in a folding chair, getting makeup applied to his cheeks by Deb. "You'd better watch out Cayden Hart," Easton laughed, pointing at Barrett. "If you don't do your job right, you're looking at your replacement."

❧ 4 ❧

"Wⁿhat the hell are you doing?" cried Lainey, dismounting from Sand and dropping the reins. The faithful gelding remained in place, trained to ground tie. Lainey marched over to Barrett with fire in her eyes.

She took a swing.

Her knuckles met his jaw hard, making his head swivel back. Shocked, Barrett teetered for a second and regained his footing from the force of her blow. He'd seen more out-of-control women than he cared to remember on the job, usually jacked up on drugs and ready for bear. But he honestly never saw this one coming from a Hollywood actress who'd seemed so sweet a mere fifteen minutes ago while she'd gotten her face powdered to "camera ready" perfection. Let alone someone who'd remembered him fondly from teen horse camp.

"How *dare* you rescue me in front of the film crew!" Lainey demanded, her fists clenched. "Do you have any idea how long I've worked for respect in this industry? I insisted in my contract that I'd do *all* my own riding and stunts." She pulled back her elbow for another slam. "And I was just about to stop that horse *myself*—"

Instinctively, Barrett blocked her arm and wrapped his elbow around her neck in a classic restraint hold, fully prepared to choke her out if he needed to. He held her body close to his chest and used his other arm to pin her hands, squeezing like a snake.

"Stop your horse, huh? Which is why she was *accelerating?*" he pointed out in a maddeningly calm tone, the one he always used on the job for dealing with crazy. Nevertheless, he couldn't help noticing the way Lainey's warm body felt against his chest—even if she was as mad as hell. Her skin and hair smelled as fresh as wildflowers, and her natural curves under the thin calico dress were nothing short of intoxicating. The more she wriggled, the tighter his arms cinched around her. Barrett couldn't resist—he leaned his chin against the crook of her neck and simply breathed her in, feeling her pulse quicken against her soft skin, all the while keeping his hold firm. He didn't want to scare her with his restraint, but he didn't exactly want to get smacked again either.

"Let go of me!" she cried, flailing her legs to try and kick him. "I can't believe I hugged you earlier! You sabotaged me—"

Barrett smirked at her boldness and curled one of his legs around hers so she couldn't get leverage—relishing the feel of being entwined with her more than he cared to admit. In the heat of the moment, they were totally wrapped up in one another, her heart beating as fast as a bird's. Barrett pressed his cheek against Lainey's and whispered in her ear, "May I remind you that you've already assaulted me once? For your information, Miss Neil, I'm a police officer. And if you don't stop trying to hurt me, I'm going to have to arrest you."

Lainey squirmed fiercely anyway, and Barrett deftly released his neck-hold and grabbed her elbow, twisting it to make her body swing with a quick flip to the ground that left her dizzied in shock. Then he bent down and pressed his knee against her back to secure his hold. Lainey wailed like a wildcat, the sound muffled by the tall grass her face was planted in. Before she knew it, Barrett had both arms pinned behind her back, when she heard a sharp click as cold metal slid over her wrists. Barrett rolled her over and sat on her knees so she couldn't kick him and shot a glance at his watch as though comparing the time it took to handcuff Lainey with his latest calf-roping score in tie-down events. A hint of a smile surfaced on his lips. Clearly, he was impressed with his results.

"I have a gun, Miss Neil," he flatly informed her, patting a bulge on his right hip hidden by the tail of his flannel shirt. "Just remember, this was the soft approach."

"B-But I'm the star!" Lainey sputtered.

"Of the nearest jail?"

Lainey's mouth dropped. "You *wouldn't!*"

"Quite the opposite—it's my job," Barrett asserted. "Unless you straighten up and stop throwing punches at law enforcement. You think being pulled off a horse was embarrassing in front of the crew? Wait till they see your mug shot." He rubbed his jaw and glared at her. "I'd be happy to show the local judge my bruise."

When it became clear Lainey had given up the idea of kicking, Barrett slid off her legs and sat cross-legged in front of her while she wriggled upright with her hands cuffed behind her back, still attempting to catch her breath. Her wrists had turned a painful pink.

"So, you're a bit sensitive about how you're perceived by that bozo director in butt-ugly boots?" Barrett glanced back at the film crew, who appeared to be milling around and at a loss for what to do since their ATVs wouldn't start. "Something tells me that crew would be cheering right now if you'd decked *him* instead of me." Another smirk settled on Barrett's lips. "But I will compliment you on your right hook, Miss Neil. Very effective."

Lainey blushed. She drew in a deep breath and studied the ground for a moment where the indentation of her face still lingered on the grass. Barrett wasn't sure, but he thought he saw tears mist in her eyes.

"I had a good teacher, remember?" She braved a glance at him. "You showed me the classic four moves: power stance— knees bent—take a step—drive the blow from your legs using your whole body. You made me practice those instructions for hours after my dad...struck me...that summer. So he'd always think twice about doing it again. Guess it kind of becomes a reflex whenever I feel, you know, threatened." Lainey checked his expression. "I, um, I never got the chance to...thank you."

She gazed into his eyes with such sincerity that it made Barrett's breath catch. He was the last man on earth ever to be called sentimental. In fact, he'd been reprimanded by the department more times than he could count for unnecessary force. But that moment when he'd defended Lainey all those years ago had been seared into his heart forever. Ever since then, he couldn't help wondering if she'd followed through with the strategies he'd shown her. Curious, Barrett leaned over for a second and peered at her hands. From the scars he spied on her knuckles, it looked like she'd put his training to good use.

When Lainey saw his reaction, she sat a little taller, lifting her chin with a defiant look.

"I got rid of him," she stated proudly. "By the time I hit sixteen—legal emancipation. My dad had thrown away all my money on bad real estate investments, of course. On top of trying to make me a punching bag for his flaws. H-He's in jail now for fraud," her voice cracked a little. "I had to pay restitution to his victims for years. But at least he can't hurt anyone anymore."

Though Lainey's tone had turned fragile, her eyes burned like a furnace.

Barrett stared at her delicate face, with more weariness than a 24-year-old should ever have, shocked to hear her life had turned out as difficult as his after that golden summer. They'd been so young then, untouched by tragedy. He couldn't have known his parents were about to die in a car crash, forcing him to go to reform school that was a unique version of hell, all because he and his brothers had gotten into scrapes with the law from their anger and grief. And she couldn't have known her abusive father had far more plans for betrayal. Their gazes locked, and in that moment, Barrett could see in her pure blue eyes the way the emotional scars still sculpted her soul, the same way they'd done to his. Nothing about them was as relaxed as it had been that summer, and

Barrett felt his heart twist over the loss of who they both used to be.

He slowly cleared his throat. "So, you're trying to recoup some of the money that your Dad squandered away by doing this film?"

Lainey shook her head. "No," she said in a clipped tone. "I'm only getting paid scale, and frankly, the real star is Cayden Hart over there." She nodded at the film crew, who had resorted to finishing their lunches until she made her way back. "Former teen heartthrob who desperately wants to break into adult film roles. Sound familiar?"

"Then why are you in this movie?"

Lainey's eyebrows tightened as she gathered her thoughts. "Because I *know* Ada Holdwell. I *am* Ada Holdwell," she insisted. "I realize that sounds crazy, but it doesn't matter how flashy my co-star is. This character, she fights to survive, and nothing's been handed to her. She's been beaten up by life."

Barrett boldly lifted her chin with his finger.

"Like you?"

His lips were dangerously close, and heat prickled Lainey's forehead and cheeks. She could never forget that horrible day at age fourteen when her father drove his palm into her face. Nor could she forget the way this handsome guy in front of her had protected her with everything he had—succeeding against someone twice his size. It was honestly the first time in Lainey's whole life that someone had made her feel…worth it. Before that, Lainey had always been a cute commodity, something her father peddled to Hollywood for money, if only she could finally be thin enough, perky enough, accommodating enough. But there was nothing perky and accommodating about her role of Ada Holdwell. She was a fighter, just like Lainey.

Lainey peered at Barrett's unbearably attractive face with high cheekbones, a chiseled jaw, and dark brown eyes that held a promise that he'd defend her all over again if given half a chance, regardless of whether she was considered Hollywood "cute." Something about the way his soulful gaze caught hers said he'd relish that opportunity.

"I'm doing this movie," she explained carefully, "because the story needs to be told. About a plain woman who gets by on pure courage. The whole stupid romance thing doesn't come till the end anyway and was just tacked on for ratings. There's real meat in Ada's story," she insisted, "something that might inspire young girls who are in the same situation I used to be in."

The determination in Lainey's eyes pierced Barrett's heart.

"Well, Miss Neil," he said, "the way I figure it, you have two options."

"Which are?" she replied, lifting a brow.

"You can apologize for assaulting me, and I'll take off your handcuffs with just a warning. Or we can head to the Bandits Hollow police station right now."

Barrett leaned in closer, making her heart skip.

"Of course, there is a third option," he smiled with a twinkle in his eye, pulling out the key to her handcuffs. He dangled it in front of her nose.

Lainey squinted at the key. "Which is?" she said, her lips firm, doing her darndest not to betray how devilishly attractive she thought he'd become when that mischievous smile surfaced on his face.

"You could let me take you to dinner this evening."

"For *hitting* you?" Stunned, Lainey studied his eyes for a moment to see if he could possibly be serious, when she spied the pure pleasure he was getting from baiting her. "Wait a minute—isn't bartering with suspects *illegal*, Officer Iron Feather?" she pointed out. "Between the two of us, we could *both* land ourselves in jail." A smirk teased at the corner of her lips, then her face broke into a wicked grin. "But hey, for allowing me a free practice session with my right hook," she gave him a sly wink and rubbed her knuckles before holding up her handcuffs for Barrett to unlock, "I won't tell if you won't."

ꙮ 5 ꙮ

L ainey sat in cowhide-covered booth beneath an elk-antler lamp in the Golden Wagon Restaurant and picked up the menu. It had literally been a decade since she'd eaten here, but the fare hadn't changed a bit—a tasty lineup of comfort foods designed to make local ranchers feel warm and welcome. Her eyes roamed over the steak platter special, when she dropped her gaze to her stomach and chewed her lip.

"You're *not* fat," Barrett insisted, as if he'd heard her thoughts. Sitting across the table from her, he gazed into her eyes. "You *never* were. As a matter of fact, if anything, you could use a few pounds. Try one of Nell's famous platters—steak, ribs, fried chicken. Might do you some good." His deep brown eyes told her he meant it.

"Old habits die hard, I guess," Lainey shrugged. "Especially when you've been told you're chubby your whole

life, and you can't remember the last time you actually finished
a meal."

"Was that Hollywood, or your dad?" asked Barrett.
"Because it sure couldn't have been any red-blooded man
around here. You're gorgeous, Lainey Neil, even without
makeup. Don't ever let anybody tell you otherwise." A slight
smile traced his lip. "But I still think you could use some extra
pounds to carry you through winter." His gaze drifted to the
creases around her eyes and on her forehead from being
underweight. "Just remember," he said, "tonight, the tab's on
me—and you don't even have to throw another right hook
my way."

In spite of Barrett's good-natured teasing, Lainey's pulse
quickened from his compliments while she kept her eyes glued
to the menu. The second she'd finished filming for the day,
she'd washed off all the movie makeup and exchanged her
prairie dress for a comfy t-shirt and jeans. The way Barrett saw
her right now wasn't Hollywood hype at all—it was the way
she really looked, as Mother Nature intended. It felt so good
for someone to appreciate her for who she genuinely was.
Lainey swept her honey-brown hair away from her face and
pretended to focus more closely on the menu, trying not to let
on that she was flattered.

"Okay," she said with resolve, "steak platter it is." A
mischievous glimmer surfaced in her eyes. "With a *loaded*
baked potato." She closed the menu and slid it to the edge of
the table. Grabbing a red bandana napkin that held a knife
and a fork, she unraveled it and set the bandana on her lap.

"Perfect. I'll have the same," replied Barrett.

After the waitress came by and took their orders, he

glanced around the room at the enormous river rock fireplace and vintage wanted posters for outlaws that hung on the walls, knowing one of them was his notorious ancestor Iron Feather. His eyes drifted to the director in a nearby booth, dining with a member of the crew and a couple of extras. He shifted his gaze back to Lainey.

"You know, something's been troubling me about filming today," he said, leaning his elbows on the table. The way his dark eyes bored into hers made her uneasy.

"Aside from Cinnamon running away with me?" Lainey replied. "I don't know what got into her. During our practice rides yesterday she was great. A little on the docile side, to be honest. I thought she was a good match for *Skystone Canyon*."

Barrett nodded, but she could tell his thoughts were preoccupied, spooling a mile a minute. He studied a few other crew members that sat in booths in the restaurant.

"What—what it is it?" pressed Lainey, noticing the trail of his gaze.

Barrett shook his head. He leaned back in the booth and folded his arms, his eyes troubled. "Did you happen to notice that none of the crew came out to the pasture to see how you were doing after Cinnamon took off?"

Lainey thought about it for a second. "Guess they assumed you'd already done the job," she shrugged. "Now that you mention it, that was a little weird."

"So were the burs on Cinnamon's saddle blanket," Barrett mentioned with a stern face. "No wonder she started bucking —the spikes on the burs must have driven her crazy. The reason the crew members didn't check on you was because their ATVs were out of gas. All they had was a cheap, two-wheel-drive truck that wouldn't have made it over the terrain. Weird is the word all right."

Lainey rolled her eyes. "I think you've been a policeman too long, Officer Iron Feather," she said. "Mishaps like that occur on sets all the time. Along with temper tantrums and ego wars. None of it means anything. In my business," she sighed, "you learn to go with the flow."

At that moment, the waitress came by with their platters. When she set them down, Lainey dug greedily into her baked potato, relishing the rich flavor of butter, sour cream, and bacon bits. She took her knife and began cutting up the steak, popping a big hunk of sirloin into her mouth. "Mm," she purred in ecstasy, "you sure don't get steak like this in Hollywood."

Barrett's eyes glinted, happy to see her eating with abandon and hoping it might alleviate the drawn look to her features. Nevertheless, his eyes narrowed. "You know," he said between chews of beef, "those burs in Cinnamon's saddle blanket weren't from around here."

To Lainey's surprise, he dug into his pocket and set a small cluster of burs on the table. They were nasty, with sharp prongs that could dig into any animal's hide and make him or her miserable. When Lainey peered closer, she realized they were surrounded by dried clover leaves.

"These are burclover," Barrett said. "I looked them up— they don't grow in the Rocky Mountains at high altitude. They're probably from California."

"All right," responded Lainey in a tolerant tone tinged with skepticism, "so they must have gotten stuck to the saddle blanket in LA, wherever the studio stored the saddles. They were probably on the ground when some crew member accidentally dropped the saddle in the dirt. It happens. No big deal."

"That's a reasonable enough explanation," Barrett admitted. "But what about the gas? I asked a crew member and he said he'd filled the ATVs the night before."

"Welcome to Hollywood!" Lainey grinned. "Don't get me wrong—I love our crew. They work their butts off. But Easton Wolfe," she lowered her voice, sneaking a glance in his direction, "expects everybody to rush around like squirrels so he can wrap the film fast and earn a big fat bonus from the studio. Without sharing any compensation with the crew, I might add. You've seen him—it's impossible to get everything done that he demands. I bet the poor guy lied about gassing up the vehicles to keep Easton off his back."

"Mail call!" rang a cheerful voice, startling Lainey. Before she knew it, Deb Griffin had slid into the booth beside her, holding up a wad of mail. She thumbed through several envelopes and pulled out a couple for Lainey. The envelope on top was postmarked from a penitentiary in California. The return address indicated it had been sent by *Inmate: Gerald Neil*.

"Ouch," Deb winced as she handed the letter to Lainey. She patted her forearm in sympathy. "Nothing like getting a personal letter from dear old dad, huh?"

"AKA Satan?" Lainey remarked with a shadow crossing over her face. Reluctantly, she tore open the envelope and sucked in a breath, bracing for the letter's contents. She turned to Deb as if this were a familiar ritual. "Ready for the latest?" she said as she prepared to read aloud. "Here goes."

Dear Lainey,

I'm on parole now in southern California. This is the last stamped envelope they gave me in the pen to let you know. Where the hell have you gone? I stopped by your apartment last night, but you weren't there. Why the bleep haven't you written back and sent me money, you bleeping bleep bleep…

Lainey glanced up at Barrett and Deb, assuming their imaginations could fill in the foul, four-letter names he'd called her. "Feel the love," she said with heavy irony, setting the letter down and gazing at the postmark. It had been sent a week ago and forwarded to her by the post office to the film set. She buried her head in her hands. "How on earth can he possibly be out on parole?" she groaned. "He was supposed to do two more years for fraud."

"Good behavior." Deb shook her head. "We both know he can turn on the charm, when it's in his interest." She gazed into Lainey's eyes with genuine concern. "But no matter what, you're going to be okay, honey. You've stood up to him before, with me by your side, and you'll stand up to him again. You're a star in more ways than one, sweetheart."

"Oh, thank you, Deb," Lainey replied, leaning over in the seat to give her a quick hug. "I don't know what I would've have done without you all these years, especially with the nightmare called my dad. You're my rock."

Deb nodded, giving her hand a squeeze. "Did you see the other envelope, the one from your agent? Maybe it's better news."

Lainey opened the gold envelope on the table with her agent's return address from Beverly Hills. To her surprise, there was no personal letter or note inside, only a formal contract with sticky-note arrows showing where to sign.

"Whoa, quite the hint, huh?" she remarked to Deb. She glanced up at Barrett. "My agent's been bugging me for a while to play the lead in a Las Vegas revue of my old TV show *Horse Feathers*. It's supposed to be a *musical*—choreographed with live horses. Wearing glitter, for Christ's sake." Lainey ran her hand through her long hair. "Of course, there are a couple of glitches with that idea. Number one, I can't sing to save my life. And number two, I'm hardly a teenager anymore." She shook her head as if the idea were preposterous.

"Well, from what you told me last month, they're offering you a ton of money," Deb noted. "And it would be steady work for the next three years." She patted her knee. "This offer won't be on the table forever, honey. Maybe you should take it more seriously?"

"Deb," Lainey sighed impatiently, "we've been over this. I know you want to see me be taken care of. You're the only real…parent…I've ever had." Lainey met Barrett's gaze. "Deb took me in when I won emancipation from my father. My mother died of an overdose after I was born," she explained, "and Deb's the only person who ever cared about me for *me*. Not for how much money I made." She turned and stared into Deb's eyes. "But I feel like playing the *Horse Feathers* role again is going backwards, not forwards. I want to be an adult actress now and maybe even a producer someday. Someone who'll bring powerful stories to life that are about more than cute teenagers. I understand it's a harder road, and you're worried about the toll it will take," she told Deb gently. "But I've had fame before—and frankly, it sucked. Projects like *Skystone Canyon* are more rewarding."

"Sounds like you have an admirable goal," Barrett observed, understanding better now why she often looked more world weary than her years. "And you're willing to tough it out for what matters. But the only problem is," he shot a glance at the director across the room, "you might not have a director for this film much longer."

"What?" replied Lainey. "What are you talking about?"

Barrett stood up from the booth and laid a fifty dollar bill on the table. With one hand, he pulled out his handcuffs, the other hand hovering over the concealed weapon at his hip. "I'm sorry to cut dinner short, ladies. But your director just tried to grope a teenage girl at that table while I was watching. And as much as I'd love to finish my steak and chat, I gotta be a policeman right now."

6

L ainey and Deb watched as Barrett marched with swift strides over to the booth to confront Easton Wolfe. When the director began to argue in his typical, over-the-top style, Barrett easily lifted him from his seat by his collar and whipped his body around in a snap, slapping handcuffs on his wrists before he could sputter another word. The teenage girl in the booth bent down her head and began to cry, shoulders heaving. Barrett motioned for the waitress to come sit beside her while he pulled out his cell phone and proceeded to make a call. Moments later, he clicked off his phone and tucked it into his back pocket, yanking on the director to walk beside him toward the restaurant exit. As soon as they reached Lainey's booth, Barrett paused.

"Keep an eye on the girl till her mother comes," Barrett said gravely. It was a command, not a request. "While I take this asshole to the station. You said you might want to become a producer someday?" He stared at Lainey. "I suggest you make calls real quick to the Wings Channel about hiring another director. 'Cause you're gonna need one, fast."

"Th-This can't be happening," Lainey stuttered in shock. But when she glanced at the poor girl sobbing beside the waitress in the booth, her heart sank.

She knew that feeling.

The same thing had happened to her once, when she auditioned for a teen cosmetics commercial. She was only 15, and her father had badgered her to do the audition, claiming it would be "lucrative." Lainey only relented to get him off her back. Yet on the way to the audition, her dad kept insisting that she "smile" till her lips hurt, because he'd heard the director was a warm, touchy-feely kind of guy.

Touchy-feely was right—

During the audition, he brazenly squeezed her breast to make her appear more "perky" in front of the camera and informed her in no uncertain terms that there were "ways" to secure a long-term contract with the brand. Then he pressured her to go to his office to discuss it on his couch.

Seriously, a *couch*?

He couldn't have been more obvious. Though Lainey elbowed him hard to break free and stormed out of the audition room to her father's car, that didn't mean she wasn't rattled.

By this time, she'd already suspected her father was mismanaging her money, but this man wanted more. The whole experience left her so shaken she missed filming the following day at *Horse Feathers*, pretending she had the flu.

Lainey had never told a soul what really happened.

Gazing at the girl breaking down in the restaurant, Lainey's heart broke for her, and she excused herself from Deb and walked with determination over to her booth.

"I'll take it from here," she instructed the waitress with a kind smile. "I'm employed with the film company."

Lainey sat down beside the girl and put her arm around her shoulder.

"You're really brave," she whispered in her ear as she rubbed her back. "It's not your fault. The same thing happened to me once. I-I know what you're going through."

The girl lifted her gaze. Her red eyes met Lainey's.

"Y-You do?" she said, lips trembling. Her face was beet red from the shock.

"I went through the same thing, when I was around your age," Lainey confessed with compassion in her tone. "I'm Lainey Neil, by the way."

"I know who you are," replied the girl. "Everybody does. You're the star—"

Lainey shook her head. "No. I'm just another girl like you, who wanted to act. And who got taken advantage of. You didn't in any way deserve this, Miss..."

"Heather," the girl replied. "I-I had no idea," she sputtered, tears brimming again. "He seemed so nice, and he offered to pay for my meal and dessert—whatever I wanted. But the minute the other two people left our booth, he put his hand on my knee and started inching toward my crotch. Then he said the most awful things. Like if I didn't go to his room right now, he'd spread all these lies about me and I'd never act again. I pushed away his hand and tried to leave the booth, but he blocked me." Her throat choked with a sob. "He kept th-threatening——"

Lainey gave the girl a huge bear hug, allowing her to wilt in her arms. "It's okay now," she whispered as she rocked her back and forth, hoping the warmth of her embrace could somehow alleviate Heather's trauma. "I *believe* you." Lainey gently stroked her hair. "The man that handcuffed the director is a police officer. He saw *everything*." Lainey lifted Heather's chin and then cupped her tear-soaked cheeks, looking into her eyes. "That director is gone for good. Do you hear me? Whoever we get for this film, you have my *word* that I'll personally watch out for you. That is, if you still want to be part of this film. I'm so sorry this happened to you."

Heather nodded and spied a middle-aged woman who'd dashed into the restaurant, her face the picture of panic. When she saw Heather, she bolted for the booth.

"Heather!" she cried.

Lainey slid out of the booth to make room for her, watching as the woman sat down and engulfed Heather in her arms. "You okay, honey? You all right?" the woman gasped, clutching her tighter. Heather nodded, glancing over at Lainey.

"This is Lainey Neil, Mom," Heather said. "She was really nice to me, after the director tried to…" her voice trailed off.

"What did he do? Did he hurt you?" the mother demanded desperately.

Heather shook her head. "H-He mostly made threats," she replied, "and I was able to push his hand away. A policeman arrested him, and Miss Neil said she'd…protect me…on the set."

"The set?" her mother blurted. "Are you kidding? Over my dead body! I don't want you to go near a set ever again—"

"I'm *staying* in the movie, Mom," Heather insisted through trembling lips. She flicked a gaze at Lainey for courage and raised her chin. "This is my dream. Ever since I was five, I've wanted to act." She checked Lainey's eyes again to bolster her resolve. "And I'm not going to let one creepy guy scare me off. He's gone now, Mom, and I want to finish."

Tears slipped down Lainey's cheeks. She folded her arms against her waist to try and maintain some semblance of control. The girl reminded her so much of herself at that age, prevailing with determination, no matter what came her way. She gave Heather a smile, wiping her cheeks. "I'm proud of you," Lainey said, uttering the words that no one had ever bothered to say to her when she was a kid. She prayed her support would make Heather realize how brave she really was. "You're a very strong girl."

Lainey leaned over to her mother and gently set her hand on her shoulder.

"As a parent, it's entirely your decision whether she returns to filming," Lainey assured her. "But if Heather wants to stay in *Skystone Canyon*, I will personally take her under my wing and make sure she's comfortable and safe, with continued police surveillance." Lainey looked Heather in the eye. "It's the least I can do."

The mother saw the unusual connection between them, the way Heather's eyes glinted with hope from her new-found bond with the film's star. She chewed her lip for a moment and hesitated.

"Okay," she finally replied with reluctance to Heather.

"But only if I can be on the set, too. All right? I know you hate having a stage mother around, but in this case, honey, I think it's warranted."

"Do you have to?" Heather pressed. "I don't want you embarrassing me by standing too close. I'm fifteen now, mom. I don't want anybody to know my mother's there."

Lainey winced. She would have given her eye teeth if her mother or father had ever come to one of her sets. But her mother was long gone, and her father simply stayed at home and waited for her to bring home checks for him to cash. Nevertheless, Lainey nodded at Heather with a sly smile.

"Be careful what you wish for," she said, giving her a wink. "Now you'll have *two* guardians looking after you—your mother and me. Oh, and a police officer to boot." She drew in a deep breath and cast a glance back at Deb, who was still waiting patiently for her in the other booth. "Which means I'd better get busy and call the Wings Channel to find another director. See you two later," she smiled with a certain trepidation in her tone. "Just as soon as we get this film rolling again."

7

"Hello, this is Lainey Neil of the *Skystone Canyon* film," she announced on the phone with as much courage as she could muster. "Could you please put me through to the producer, Harper Stone?"

"Yes, Ms. Neil," replied the pleasant receptionist. "Hang on a moment while I track her down."

Heart in her throat, Lainey listened to a bland melody while she was placed on hold, waiting for the woman to come to the phone who was renowned throughout Hollywood for being carved from pure ice.

Harper Stone—beautiful, brilliant, and born with a deadly tongue.

Harper was famous for eating actors and crew members for breakfast with her brutal good looks and the kind of brassy sarcasm that could make Bette Davis stand up and cheer from her grave. She'd forged a career as a blonde bombshell with a steel rod up her back in TV dramas, but at the age of 45, the roles weren't coming like they used to, so she'd been struggling to create a career as a producer. *Skystone Canyon* was her first film for the Wings Channel.

"Lainey?" said the chirpy receptionist from the other end. "I've located Ms. Stone now and I'm about to transfer you. Hold on."

Lainey could hear the cold telephone rings, and she braced herself to deal with relaying the bad news to Harper about the film's director.

"This is Harper Stone," said the producer in a clipped tone. "Whatever it is, belt it out now, because I don't have any extra goddamned time for waiting around."

Lainey's words stifled in her throat. She'd never heard anyone answer a phone call like that. Clock ticking, she came to her senses, releasing a torrent of words.

"Ms. Stone, I'm Lainey Neil. You know, from the *Skystone Canyon* movie? Listen, Easton Wolfe blew it big time. He was in a local restaurant where there was an undercover cop who does security for the set, and he propositioned a teenage girl. Easton, I mean, not the police officer. He tried to grope her and pressure her to go to his room. The policeman saw everything—and holy cow—he got arrested right then and there—"

Lainey felt like a fool, her words spilling out of control. She couldn't help it. She was nervous about divulging the scandalous details to Harper, and the dead silence on the other end only aggravated her nerves. For all she knew, Harper could shelve the whole film and call it quits. Lainey waited patiently, feeling every second tick by while the line remained quiet. Finally, Harper broke her silence.

"Why are *you* calling me, instead of the assistant director?"

"B-Because I can't find him," Lainey admitted, her pulse quickening. "I think he quit and skipped town."

Lainey winced, knowing that didn't sound good.

At all.

After the news of the incident tore through the film crew like wildfire, the assistant director, who was known for being slavishly loyal to Easton, had apparently ditched the project. What were the odds that Harper would want to keep it going? To make matters worse, Harper's silence seemed interminable.

"Am I to understand," Harper broke the dead air in a grave tone, "that Easton Wolfe is now in…jail?"

"Um, yeah," Lainey fumbled, "I mean, he was carted off in handcuffs. I assume that's where the policeman was headed."

Silence again.

Lainey could have sworn a full minute passed by without Harper saying a word.

"Oh…thank…God!" Harper burst, to Lainey's surprise. "It's about fricking time! I should have placed bets in Vegas for when that loser was going to get his ass thrown into the clink— I would've made a fortune. I never wanted to hire that idiot, but the studio forced me. Do me a favor, Ms. Neil. Inform the *Skystone Canyon* crew that I will be on the set at precisely eight AM tomorrow. I expect everyone to be ready for filming. Oh, and Ms. Neil?"

"Yes?" replied Lainey, still grappling with the shock of Harper's response.

"I like red velvet cake. And Bourbon. *Very* good Bourbon."

"Uh, okay?" Lainey replied uncertainly. She had no clue what Harper might be referring to.

"That means have plenty of red velvet cake and Bourbon available on the set. Do you know why?"

Lainey shook her head, her thoughts racing. "No," she replied honestly. "Not really."

"Because we're throwing a goddamned party!" Harper informed her. "And then you and I are going to roll up our sleeves and work our asses off to save this film."

🪷 8 🪷

A black stretch limousine rolled through the old western town of Bandits Hollow, kicking up clouds of dust. It slowly came to a halt at the *Skystone Canyon* set at the edge of town, its dark, tinted windshield reflecting the golden hues of the rising sun. Though the crew had been hustling to get everything ready for filming that morning, at that moment the set fell into a hush. Everyone waited in silence for Harper Stone to exit the vehicle.

Lainey stood in her calico prairie dress, squinting at the limousine. She flicked a gaze in Barrett's direction, already astride his buckskin horse and ready to keep any errant bull—or predatory director—from the cast and crew. The sight of him, tall and devastatingly handsome in the saddle with his black cowboy hat and aviator sunglasses on, took Lainey's breath away. But Barrett's presence also bolstered her courage. A cop like him would never be intimidated by the likes of

Harper Stone, Lainey thought, and she inhaled a deep breath while reminding herself of that fact over and over.

Harper's just another woman in the film industry like me, Lainey resolved, swallowing hard as she waited for signs of life from the limousine. Okay, so she has the power to nix this film in a nanosecond like it never existed. But she wouldn't have come all the way from LA unless she was serious about saving *Skystone Canyon*, right?

The back door of the limousine slowly creaked open, and out slid a graceful leg that seemed to go on for miles. Setting a black, high-heeled shoe on the ground, Harper Stone emerged, all five-feet-ten of her, dressed in a black, slim-fitting jacket and a matching pencil skirt as though she'd been cast in a film noir role. Her blonde hair was perfectly coifed like a Hollywood siren and her classically beautiful face was unreadable in large, dark sunglasses. Harper stood and folded her arms, taking her time to scan the crew members and actors dressed in pioneer clothing, when her gaze fell upon Barrett, sitting on his buckskin horse.

"Well yippee-ki-yay!" she crowed, removing her sunglasses. A slight curl lifted her crimson lips. "My God, it's refreshing to see a good-looking cowboy in the morning. Now where the hell is my Bourbon and red velvet cake?"

The limousine rolled away as a gopher dashed to bring her a piece of cake and a glass of Bourbon. Harper lifted the glass to her lips and threw her head back for a hefty swallow, then grasped the slice of cake and stuffed a corner into her mouth. She replaced the items back on the tray, licking the blood-red crumbs from her lips.

"You," she pointed abruptly at Lainey. "Who are you?"

"I-I'm Lainey Neil," she replied. "We spoke on the phone—"

"Thought so," Harper cut her off. "Come with me and show me the script for the next scene we're going to film. Oh, and have some cake and Bourbon, darling. That goes for everyone, by the way." She gestured at a large box marked *Breckenridge Bourbon Whiskey* on the ground beside a restaurant cart featuring a huge red velvet cake. On the cake was inscribed in frosting: *Happy trails, Easton. Hope you look good in orange.*

"What's with all the stone faces?" Harper railed at the actors and crew. "Get your asses over here and party! Easton's gone and it's high time to rock and roll by making a good film for a change."

Laughter erupted from the crowd along with a few hoots and cheers. The relief on the faces of the actors and crew was palpable as they lined up at the restaurant cart for cake and drinks, regardless of the early morning hour. Before Lainey knew it, Harper had linked her elbow through her arm and was practically dragging her to portable desk where there was a stack of scripts and a storyboard easel beside it.

"All right, pioneer girl," Harper barked, shoving a script into her hand. "Show me the scene we're on, because I'm your new director. The studio demanded I hire Easton because he was a name, no matter how badly he would've botched this project. Now they're going to get *Skystone Canyon* the way I originally envisioned it—within budget to boot."

Lainey flipped through the pages until she landed on the part of the story where Ada Holdwell drives a wagon team of horses while being chased by nefarious cattle rustlers, only to be saved by the male protagonist Nate Proctor. Pausing for a moment, she rolled her eyes. This was the part of the film where her entire job was to appear helpless and pretty—but not *too* pretty—as a backdrop for actor Cayden Hart to become more famous. She gritted her teeth and handed the script to Harper.

"Oh, Lord have mercy," Harper studied the upcoming scene and frowned, "how's that simpleton who used to be in a boy band supposed to pull off heroics?" She glanced back at Cayden Hart in sweatpants and an artfully torn t-shirt, lounging in a chair while eating cake, not even dressed properly and ready for the shoot. "Look," Harper whispered to Lainey, "I pressured the studio to buy this script because of the way it portrayed a strong woman who perseveres. I had no control over the casting—it was between two pop singers and a former child actor just out of rehab. Frankly, baby-faced Cayden belongs in a crib—not in a historical film about tough pioneers. We'll indulge him with a few close-ups in this scene to make the studio heads happy, then get back to focusing on your character."

All at once, Harper gripped Lainey hard by the shoulders and stared her in the eye. "So you'd better impress the hell out of me, pioneer girl. Or I'm scrapping this film."

Lainey's heart began to race. She was beyond thrilled to hear about Harper's dedication to the story, and she hoped with everything in her that she could meet—and maybe even exceed—Harper's expectations, justifying her faith in the film. To her surprise, Barrett came to her side in a shot, leaving his horse ground tied in the nearby pasture. He hovered protectively next to Lainey and glared at Harper.

"Mind removing your hands from Miss Neil's shoulders —*now*," he stated. It was an order, not a question. His tall stature and broad chest made for quite the imposing presence as his tan, chiseled face looked down on Harper in his aviator sunglasses, intimidating even the formidable Hollywood icon. Harper's breath hitched, and she removed her hands with a slight step back. Suddenly, it occurred to Lainey that Barrett might have thought she'd been propositioning an actor, just like Easton had done. After all, Hollywood predators came in many stripes. Lainey smirked a little, secretly enjoying Barrett's shielding instinct.

"Harper was just informing me about how important this film is to her," Lainey explained, giving Barrett a nod. She turned to Harper. "This is the police officer who nabbed Easton Wolfe."

"Cop *and* cowboy?" Harper waved her hand in front of her face. "My, my—this film set is getting hotter by the second!" She turned to the rest of the film crew. "*Skystone Canyon* actors and crew," she belted, in no need of a megaphone like Easton Wolfe, "prepare to film scene five!"

As soon as Harper issued her command to get ready to film, the crew brought over an old-fashioned wagon led by two horses in harnesses. The sight made Lainey recall fond memories, and she glanced at Barrett.

"Remember the time you showed me how to drive a team," she asked, "all those years ago?"

Barrett's face remained stone, as though he were still concerned about the way Harper had seized Lainey's shoulders. His silence seemed to hold actual weight while he maintained a fixed stare on Harper—a threatening reminder to leave Lainey alone. Then he slowly removed his sunglasses and folded them, slipping them into his front shirt pocket. When he turned to Lainey, she caught a distinct glint in his eye.

"As I recall," a smile teased at his lips, "you jackknifed the wagon tongue, and I had to hop on one of the horses to move the team forward and get you unstuck. That was the *first* time I rescued you, Miss Neil. Yesterday on Cinnamon was the second." He gave her a wink. "Not that I'm keeping track."

Lainey bit back a giggle. "Why on earth did they insist on teaching me to drive a wagon at horse camp, anyway? As if riding for hours wasn't enough to create callouses on my hands and butt, not to mention make me drop a few pounds."

To Lainey's astonishment, Barrett leaned close beside her ear, and she caught a whiff of the leathery pine scent that lingered on the earthy smell of his skin. The fragrance was intoxicating, and it brought back reminiscences of the handsome boy she'd met that summer who'd stolen her first kiss. Who'd sworn on his life that he cared about her and never, ever wanted to see her go. But how could she trust the sentiments of mere adolescents? Year after year she'd sent Barrett faithful letters, never to get a single one in return. Over time, it became heartbreakingly obvious that he'd moved on. And besides, they were totally different people now—from different worlds. But damned if Barrett's scent and the proximity of his disarming good looks didn't get under Lainey's skin, just like they did when she was fourteen, making tingles chase into places that brought a blush to her cheeks.

"They taught you to drive to test your *mettle*," Barrett whispered in Lainey's ear, sending goosebumps down her neck. "Because I told them, way down deep—beneath your child star reputation—I could tell you had grit. It was in your eyes all along, Lainey, and in your heart. Ray, the ranch owner, figured if you could conquer driving a team of wayward horses, you could conquer just about anything."

More goosebumps skittered across Lainey's skin. The

summer's activities had done exactly that: they'd given her the strength to deal with her dad—and with Hollywood. With his gentle instruction and protective advice, even at the age of fourteen, so had Barrett Iron Feather. Every time she encountered an obstacle on the ranch that seemed impossible, he patiently showed her how to overcome it by drawing on her courage and listening to her heart. For the first time in her life, Lainey had caught a glimpse of how to become the guardian of her own soul.

But the pain of Barrett never bothering to contact her again still ached more than Lainey wanted to admit...

At that moment, a sleek black horse with a western saddle was led beside them, jolting Lainey from her memories. She spied Cayden sitting on a folding chair and talking on a cell phone with a Bourbon in his hand, still in his sweats. He appeared oblivious to the fact that this was his horse and they were about to film a scene.

"Cayden Hart!" Harper called out in a stringent tone. "Get your damn jeans and cowboy boots on—you're up!"

Cayden rolled his eyes and set down his drink, ending his call. In front of everyone, he peeled off his sweats and tossed them aside to put on a pair of jean and boots and slipped a western shirt over his torn t-shirt. Then he walked up to the black horse and waited for the crew to bring a small stepstool in order to assist him into the saddle. When he finally mounted the horse, he fumbled with the reins like they were made of spaghetti.

Barrett shot Lainey a sharp look. "*That's* the hero of your film?" he remarked, floored. "Better keep your chin up and a tight hand on those reins, Miss Neal." Shaking his head, he made his way back over to his horse and got in the saddle, keeping an eye on the nearby cattle.

Lainey climbed into the wagon and did as Barrett said, recalling the driving tips he'd confided a decade ago: Lace the reins between your pinky and ring fingers with your thumbs up. Get rid of any slack and always keep your elbows bent. Use the strength in your shoulders to stop or turn horses, not your arms. That's where the power is. And talk to the horses. Remember, you're a team, one unit. The team that thinks together, moves together, and won't get in trouble.

"All right," Harper directed, motioning for the crew to drive the cameras forward on dollies while a truck with a camera mounted in the bed pulled ahead of Lainey's wagon to catch her image from the front, "in scene five, Ada Holdwell drives her wagon through that meadow while angry cattle rustlers are in hot pursuit. Then Nate Proctor arrives on the scene from the other direction to save Ada. He gallops up to her wagon and stops the horses, then pulls Ada out. After that, he turns over the wagon as a shield to protect them both and begins shooting successfully at the renegades." Harper nodded at the three men on horseback portraying cattle rustlers who rode up beside the cameras. "Ready everyone? We're going to give Ada a head start and have the cattle rustlers start gaining on her, then send in Nate from the side. Crew members—make sure your bluetooths and walkie talkies are on."

An assistant stepped forward to snap the slate for scene five, and Harper cried "Roll 'em!" Lainey commanded her horses to walk, then as soon as they reached a comfortable moving rhythm, she gave the command to trot. As the horses gained speed, she urged them to break into a full-blown gallop.

Lainey's heart pounded hard, even though she'd practiced driving this wagon a dozen times prior to filming. Navigating over the bumpy terrain, she could hear the gunshots of the men playing cattle rustlers behind her, and it was easy to stay in character by appearing anxious as she endeavored to maintain control of the reins. Up ahead, the camera stationed in the flatbed of the moving truck was capturing the whole scene. It was only supposed to be thirty seconds before the crew sent in Cayden on his horse from the side to come galloping up and stop her team, but he hadn't showed. Confused, Lainey squinted at the men in the camera truck for further directions. To her surprise, the truck slowed and came to a stop.

Lainey pulled up her horses with a long, drawn-out "whoa," remembering to use her shoulder strength and lean back with the reins. When the team came to a standstill, she slid to the side of her seat and looked behind the wagon, only to see Cayden flailing on the ground in the meadow. His saddled horse was a few feet away, nibbling the grass.

The driver of the truck hopped out and marched to her wagon.

"Didn't Cayden practice riding?" he complained. "For crying out loud! He bragged to everybody that he was an expert."

Lainey shrugged. Like the rest of the crew, she didn't have much to do with prima donna Cayden, avoiding him whenever possible. One of the cameramen stepped out of the back of the truck and met up with them.

"Good grief!" he laughed, removing the bluetooth from his ear. "I've never heard a woman curse like that in my whole

life." He returned the headphone to his ear and cringed. "Well
guys, first Harper wants to stab Cayden in the heart for lying
about his riding skills, then leave him outside to die so vultures
can pick his bones. Then she wants the cop to do the riding in
this scene." He listened carefully for a moment. "She says
she'll direct the cameras when he rides out to capture the
action, and we'll film him without full face shots from our
position when it comes time for him to turn over the wagon."
His eyebrow arched and he busted out with a laugh. "Oops, I
guess there's a pretty big condition for all of this."

"Which is?" asked Lainey, shocked that they'd managed to
con Barrett into appearing in the film at all.

The cameraman shifted his gaze and appraised her with a
sparkle in his eye. "The cop says he'll only do it if you agree to
go out to dinner with him again, since last night got cut short."
He grinned and threw a thumb's up for Harper and Barrett to
see. "Way to go, dude! Okay—you're on!"

"Wait, I didn't agree to anything!" protested Lainey.

"Yeah you did. Because I want to get this scene over and
done with before nightfall. Have you ever worked with Cayden
Hart before?" He shook his head and pointed at the actor, who
was still in the meadow attempting to get back on his horse,
only to fall each time he managed to slip his foot in the stirrup.
"The guy takes forever to finish anything. And from the looks
of it, he's not going to learn to ride any time soon. So let's get
a move on with the cop, shall we? We're on a tight budget
here."

"What?" Lainey said, flabbergasted. "You can't trade me
around as a reward like a baseball card! Give me that—"

She ripped the bluetooth from the cameraman's ear.

"Harper?" she said angrily, refusing to be intimidated by the woman's haughty reputation this time. "Put the policeman on the line right now. I want to give him a piece of my mind for treating me like bait."

"No," Harper flatly replied, her tone frozen. "First of all, we need him to finish the action scenes because I don't have the time or budget to bring in extra stuntmen from LA. And second, I don't take orders from actors—period. So if you ever try this again, you're fired. And third, if you don't go out with that goddamned cowboy cop tonight, *I will*. I strongly suggest you buck up, pioneer girl."

Lainey's face flushed the bright color of the truck's tail lights. She swallowed her pride and sheepishly avoided the cameraman's gaze, knowing she'd been put in her place —big time.

"Looks like you're going out to dinner tonight, ain't ya?" the cameraman jeered good-naturedly. He grinned far too wide for Lainey's comfort level.

"Watch your step," Lainey snapped. "The last time I went out with this guy, somebody got arrested." She narrowed her eyes at the cameraman. "Which officially makes me Calamity Jane of this film. And you don't want to be next."

T hat afternoon, Lainey and Harper and the crew gathered around a monitor to watch the dailies. The digital imaging technician started up the scene that began with Lainey's team of horses in full gallop, with fear strewn across her face as shots were fired in the air from actors playing cattle rustlers.

Deb Griffin nudged Lainey with her elbow and smiled. "You look beautiful, honey," she whispered in a proud voice.

"Aw, thanks, Deb," Lainey replied, giving her arm a squeeze. "But I want to look *authentic*, not pretty. We need to be careful about the amount of powder and mascara."

The screen shot soon switched to a rider on a black horse tearing across the meadow. Though you couldn't see his face, the camera caught Barrett as he barreled up to Lainey's wagon and grabbed the reins to stop her horses. Then he jumped from his mount and ran up to the wagon, yanking her from the front seat.

Lainey rubbed her arm, still sore from the force of Barrett's brute strength. She watched on the monitor as Barrett tipped over the wagon like it was nothing and pulled her to the ground to hide behind it, all the while firing his gun at oncoming riders. After the cattle rustlers continued to advance and reached the wagon, Lainey visibly cringed when she saw Barrett boldly leap from the wagon to knock a rider off his horse. He did the same with the other two riders until all three were lying on the ground, hogtied from ropes that had been attached to his saddle. Barrett had gone against Harper's directions entirely and simply handled the situation as though it were really happening, combining his seasoned law enforcement skills with his talents for roping and tying at break-neck speed. Lainey glanced at a couple of the actors who'd been on horseback, noticing the bruises and bandages on their faces and wrists, and she feared what Harper might be about to say.

"Hot damn! That's BRILLIANT!" cried Harper, clasping her hands. "Wait till the studio sees this. Easton who? They won't even remember his name! Where is that hot cowboy, anyway?"

She slid a gaze past the cameras and equipment, spying Barrett once again astride his tall horse Sand, guarding the crew from the nearby cattle. Clearly, he had no interest at all in how he might be perceived on film, nor did he appear particularly rattled from the rough action scene. Lainey stared at him in awe of his casual demeanor, wondering if he ever got shook up by anything.

"Don't you think the policeman upstaged you a bit today?" Deb whispered to Lainey, nodding at the monitor. "After all, you're the star. With all that explosive action, the attention's on him. You're second fiddle."

"Better a rocking fight scene than Cayden's spoiled baby face," Lainey replied. "These are supposed to be rugged pioneers. He never even managed to get on his horse. Where is Cayden, by the way?"

"In the trailer," Deb sighed, "calling half a dozen women, like usual. Listen, if you need a timely rescue from having to go out to dinner with Mr. Policeman tonight, I can come up with some kind of...emergency. You know, a makeup and lighting screen test for filming tomorrow. Or maybe a wardrobe check."

Lainey heaved a deep breath. "Thanks, Deb. But I'm afraid I got conscripted this time—by Harper, no less. She'd probably kill me if I don't follow through. Guess she needs Barrett for the rest of the action scenes to save the film money. Did you know we met as teenagers? He actually used to be a great guy—he helped me a lot back then. I don't really know what he's like anymore. I haven't heard from him in years."

Deb's eyes grew wide. "Seriously? You used to be *friends*? He seems so gruff and unapproachable now, like he might bite." She gazed in amazement at Barrett on his horse, scanning the cattle herd as though his thoughts were a million miles from making movies. "Well, be careful of those law enforcement types," she warned. "I've heard stories that they're pretty macho, and don't treat women much better than the likes of Easton Wolfe."

"Yes, mother," Lainey teased in an impatient tone. "I know

you're looking out for me. May I remind you that I'm twenty-four years old?"

Deb smiled. "Sweetie, you'll always be a kid in my book. One who could use a little extra support. I can't help looking out for you—it's second instinct."

"You have a good heart," Lainey whispered, setting her hand on her shoulder.

"That's a wrap for today, folks!" Harper announced, gazing at her diamond-crusted Rolex as the afternoon sun began to wane on the horizon. "Meet back here tomorrow at eight in the morning, sharp!"

Lainey swiftly scanned the crew packing up to leave the set to make sure Heather was being accompanied by her mother and in good hands. The similarity between her and Deb was not lost on her, and she smiled at the girl and her mother, giving them a kindly wave. In that moment, Lainey felt a kinship with Deb for wanting to protect the girl, and she turned to her with a deeper understanding of her mother hen impulses. "I'll let you know how dinner with the cowboy cop goes tonight, okay?" Lainey assured Deb. "And if anybody else gets arrested."

"Aw, have fun and don't let him intimidate you," Deb encouraged, picking up her makeup utensils. She carefully placed them inside her cosmetics case and closed the lid. "See you tomorrow," she said as she headed off the set.

As soon as Deb exited the filming area, Barrett approached Lainey while leading two saddled horses.

"Ready for some chow?" His face broke into a crooked smile, his deep brown eyes shining like he'd won a bet. "Don't worry, we aren't heading to the Golden Wagon Restaurant again to make more arrests."

"Does that mean you're promising not to handcuff anybody?"

"I didn't say that," Barrett replied. He handed her the reins to a vibrant chestnut horse the color of flames, which tossed its nose in the air with pride. "This is my brother Dillon's horse, *Hayiitka*."

"Hi-what?"

"It means sunrise in Apache," Barrett said, stroking the horse's neck. "I wouldn't normally offer to let someone ride Dillon's horse, with the kind of power and speed *Hayiitka* has. But I figured you might still remember some of the things I taught you in horse camp."

Lainey braced herself, remaining poker faced.

At this point, she felt she had a right to appear a bit detached. On the one hand, Barrett had seemed thrilled to see her again in Bandits Hollow. And heaven knows, with his broad shoulders, muscled chest, and chiseled face, he was even sexier than she remembered. But on the other hand, he was the very same guy who'd never kept in touch with her through the years, like he'd promised.

Why the attention now? Lainey wondered. Do I simply seem like an easy mark?

With good looks that far surpass Cayden Hart's, Lainey thought, lassoing women must be a breeze for Barrett Iron Feather. Has he changed from the kind, sincere boy of my memories? The one who once said I was his first kiss, too?

Yet the truth was, when it came to the things Barrett had

taught her at horse camp, Lainey had remembered every
single word…

How could she not, when his horse experience turned out
to be the best advice ever for dealing with her dad as well?

*Always anticipate what a horse is going to do before he does it, so
you'll never be broadsided.*

*Make the decision that you're the alpha in this situation. You're the
herd leader who decides the action, rather than reacting all the time.*

*Keep your head up, your heels down, and don't ever take any guff. If
you demand respect, you'll be amazed at how other creatures respond
in kind.*

Those words were emblazoned on Lainey's brain from the
time she was fourteen as surely as if Barrett had used a
branding iron. The cool way Barrett never showed fear, even
back then, had been an example to Lainey for how she could
live her life proud. Whether it was a squirrelly horse, or her
abusive father and all of the Hollywood users that blew
through her life—those instructions had become words to live
by. Along with the biggest example Barrett had shown her that
didn't have a damn thing to do with words:

*Sometimes, you have to hit back with all you've got to let them know
exactly who they're dealing with.*

Lainey nodded her head, recalling the image of her father
flattened in the dirt of a horse corral a decade ago. "Yeah, I
think I remember some of what you showed me," she replied,
using her best acting skills to seem nonchalant. "But why do
we need horses to go to dinner?"

"Because," Barrett said, stepping into the stirrup and
swinging into Sand's saddle, "we're heading to a cookout."

Lainey tilted her head, puzzled. "A cookout? You mean outdoors?"

"Better get on *Hayiitka* quick," Barrett nodded. "Before I break Sand into a gallop and that horse drags you by the reins to keep up. Believe me, Dillon's horse *never* likes to be left behind."

11

L ainey felt like she was flying. The extraordinary chestnut galloped beneath her, covering an impossible amount of ground as they advanced over a pasture in the direction of the dipping sun. *Hayiitka's* powerful muscles churned in rhythm with his strides, making it obvious that not only did he hate to be left behind, he was also as competitive as hell. Though Sand was a champion roping horse many times over, *Hayiitka* was determined to thrust his nose out ahead of him while drumming his hooves against the earth with a vengeance. The chestnut's long, flame-colored mane lashed against Lainey's face, making her cheeks sting, yet all she could do was smile.

Honestly, she couldn't remember the last time she'd had this much fun.

In that moment, a thousand miles from Hollywood, the majestic chestnut made her feel like she could kiss the sky.

Impulsively, she looped her reins around the saddle horn, giving *Hayiitka* his full head for a second so she could stretch out her arms like wings. Though she still had on her prairie dress from filming that day, she felt as free as a bird.

Barrett spied her unbridled joy, and his face slipped into a smile.

"Missed this, did ya?" he called out. "I must say, Miss Neil, for the first time since I've seen you again in Bandits Hollow, you actually look…happy. Instead of bracing yourself all the time to, you know, survive work."

"You should talk!" Lainey fired back, gathering up her reins. "Playing policeman day and night, whether you're still on the set or not?" A wicked look arose in her eyes, and she pressed her legs against *Hayiitka* to urge him to race ahead of Sand. After several bounding strides, a rope suddenly landed and cinched around her horse's neck, holding him back from gaining the lead.

"Not so fast!" Barrett cried, pushing Sand to charge ahead of *Hayiitka*. "You forgot how well I rope." As soon as Sand advanced a length ahead, Barrett dropped the end of his rope and goaded his horse into overdrive, leaving Lainey and *Hayiitka* in the dust.

Lainey coughed for a moment and pulled up her horse, waving away the dust clouds. Then she spotted Barrett and Sand by an enormous granite wall of boulders, gleaming in the afternoon sun. It appeared that their trail options had ended.

Lainey tightened her legs, breaking *Hayiitka* into a canter to catch up with them. "Where's the cookout supposed to be?" she asked, glancing around. She pointed toward a familiar dirt road on the left that cut through a dark grove of trees. "The forest road over there goes past a box canyon where there's an old cabin that we're using for filming." She scanned the large boulders against a mountainside that appeared impenetrable. "Why are you next to those rocks? Did you lose the trail or something?"

"No," Barrett replied, "but most people do. That's the point."

He nodded at the dirt road she'd mentioned. "That's the old stagecoach route," he said, "from over a century ago, when they used to transport gold to the banks in Florence. My ancestor Iron Feather and his gang robbed those stagecoaches as well as trains." He gazed at the boulders beside him as if they held a mysterious portal. "We're taking his secret escape trail north instead that will save us over an hour to the cookout. It's called the Thieves Trail, known only to the Bandits Hollow Gang—and a few of their descendants." His lip curled upward. "Like me."

Lainey shuddered.

She'd heard legends about the Bandits Hollow Gang from roasting marshmallows late at night around a fire back in her horse camp days. Apparently, they'd been the scourge of the Colorado mining industry in the nineteenth century, their tactics shrouded in mystery—and magic. Barrett's Native American ancestor wasn't simply an outlaw. Iron Feather was also considered a renowned medicine man, one who possessed…special powers. Some people in Bandits Hollow claimed his presence was still around in the form of animal messengers that manifested as his familiars.

To her surprise, Lainey saw Barrett and Sand vanish

around the large boulders. She blinked twice, detecting no apparent trail at all. When she urged her horse nearer to the rocks and peeked around the other side, she spotted Sand climbing a steep grade up ahead, stepping as gingerly as a mountain goat on the rocky hillside and sending stones tumbling down with every strike of his hooves. The path appeared so precarious that it made Lainey's breath hitch, and she gripped the saddle horn with all her might as *Hayiitka* surged after them, leaving her wondering how they could possibly navigate this trail without sliding. To make matters worse, another huge boulder blocked the narrow trail several yards ahead. Only this time, it was flanked by steep rock cliffs, making the way forward impossible. Undaunted, Barrett kept advancing until he reached the rock and halted his horse.

All at once, the voice of a great horned owl ripped through the air, making an eerie echo bounce off the cliffs as though the rocks themselves were chiming in on its call. A breeze began to rifle Lainey's long hair and the nearby aspens, making the leaves skitter with the sound of dry whispers. Lainey couldn't explain it, but she had the unnerving feeling they were being *watched*. From the corner of her eye, she spied the silhouette of an owl with its wings outstretched flying over the boulder that blocked their way. Yet when she glanced up, she couldn't find a single bird in the sky. Puzzled, her eyes dropped back to the boulder, where the silhouette had mysteriously changed.

It now resembled the shadow of a man—

Barrett hopped off his horse and turned to her with a stern gaze.

"You are never to tell anyone about this trail," he warned. "Do you understand?"

"W-Why's that?" Lainey stammered. "Is it, like, cursed or something?"

"Depends on who you are," Barrett replied. "My ancestor Iron Feather was a famous tracker. He had a mysterious way of making sure the wrong people didn't follow him. Some say he continues to track souls to this day." He glanced at the heavy shadow against the rock. "It's best not to tempt fate."

Lainey's throat tightened, her heart pumping too hard for comfort. She'd wanted to ask Barrett how he intended to keep going on this blocked trail, but at that moment, she couldn't force out the words. Shaking her head, she noticed the silhouette of the man remained against the granite like a stain, as though it were a sign of a sentry guarding the old trail. She shot a glance over her shoulder to see if the shadow might have come from a thick ponderosa, but the hillside only held spindly aspens. Swallowing hard, she gestured at the boulder ahead.

"Barrett, what's the point of bringing me on this trail from hell, if we're trapped?"

To her surprise, Barrett picked up a log from the ground and rammed it at the base of the boulder, where it stuck up at a thirty-degree angle like a toothpick. "Because *trapped* is only an illusion, something my ancestor knew well. But then again, they say he always did have a knack for slipping through... dimensions. C'mon," he motioned for her to join him on the ground, "help me with this log."

Curious, Lainey nudged *Hayiitka* forward and dismounted when she reached Barrett. All at once, he boldly picked her up by the waist and gently set her down on the log. When he situated himself beside her, the log began to sink lower to the ground like one end of a teeter totter. Lainey heard a deep rumbling sound, and she realized their combined weight had forced the boulder to budge a few inches. Proud of himself, Barrett glanced into her eyes and held out his hand.

"May I have this dance, Miss Neil?" he requested, standing to his feet on the log. "I have to admit, you look quite lovely in that yellow dress at sunset."

Lainey's mouth dropped. Had he lost his mind?

Despite her shock, the insistent look on Barrett's face encouraged her to rise to her feet. When she became unsteady, he swiftly grabbed her by the shoulders to help her keep her balance.

"Please don't tell me we're going to do a log roll right now," Lainey gasped, struggling to stay upright. "I realize I may look like a pioneer chick in this dress. But believe me, I have absolutely no experience with frontier pastimes."

"It's okay—I'll keep you steady," Barrett replied, his eyes gleaming. He boldly wrapped his arms around her and pulled her close—so close she was once again engulfed in that heavenly scent of his skin, her heart beating hard against her calico dress. She fluttered her eyes for a second, trying to ignore his lips that were dangerously close to kissing distance. Why, oh why, she thought, struggling against the heat that rose to her cheeks, does he have to be so goddamned handsome?

"Barrett Iron Feather," Lainey said flatly, attempting to stifle her response to the dreamy way she felt in his strong arms, made all the worse by his ridiculous physical hotness, "you've certainly got the weirdest ideas *ever* for going on a dinner date."

Barrett laughed a little. The wicked smile that lit up his face only made him all the more delicious in her eyes, forcing her to wince. "Ready?" he said. "Time to dance."

Lainey brows knit together. "Look, Barrett—I've ridden horses, driven wagons and even shot guns in the name of movie making," she confessed, eyeing the six-inch wide log warily. "But no one's ever asked me to do fancy moves on some backwoods balance beam in the name of a good time." Her foot slipped a little, and she let out a yelp. Even though Barrett quickly caught her, she breathed hard as if she were on the verge of a panic attack. "In case you haven't noticed," Lainey burst in a resentful tone, "this isn't exactly fun anymore."

"Isn't it?" he teased, guiding her to take a step back anyway. Just as efficiently, Barrett pulled her forward as well. He repeated the action, again and again, his thick arms keeping her balanced until they were engaged in a makeshift waltz, with only the low tones of the breeze through the trees for soft, background music. Within a few seconds, however, a deep, grinding noise erupted arose from the earth behind Lainey. When she glanced back, she noticed that the boulder had…shifted.

The pressure of their movements on the log had acted like a jack, rolling the rock from the trail by several feet. Before them on the hillside now was a clear path that led up to a ridge, with no obstructions in sight.

"Bravo!" Barrett congratulated her. "Now let's get the horses."

Scooping Lainey up in his arms, he leaped to the ground

with a smug grin on his face. Then he walked over to *Hayiitka* and gallantly hoisted her into the saddle. Afterwards, he grabbed both horses' reins and led their mounts on the trail beyond the boulder. When he was finished, he dropped the reins and went back to seize the log, heading around the other side of the boulder to shove the massive rock into place, blocking entrance from the other side. With the ease in which his strong muscles managed the boulder, Lainey wondered if he really needed her help to move it in the first place, or if this had just been his bizarre idea of flirting?

Either way she looked at it, she couldn't stop thinking about the wonderful sensation of being held in his arms, even if it was only for a few moments. For a young woman who'd spent her whole life chasing the fleeting approval of directors and producers in Hollywood, those brief seconds had felt secure and downright...comforting...as though she'd finally found...

Home.

Lainey shook her head, trying to dispel such a foreign notion that did nothing but pierce her heart and make her feel vulnerable, something she rarely risked in order to keep her head above water in life. She watched while Barrett swung back into his saddle and headed up the steep trail, motioning for her to follow. Soon, they were at the top of a magnificent ridge with a 360-view of the surrounding peaks. The vista took Lainey's breath away, and she pulled up her horse to soak in the enormity of sky and the jagged backbone of the nearby mountains. Pressing her hand against her heart, she let out a gasp.

"Oh, Barrett," she gushed, "it's gorgeous up here!"

For a moment, Lainey forgave him for his peculiar impromptu dance and the strenuousness of the trail.

"And look!" She pointed to a small box canyon wedged into one of the valleys below, flanked at the entrance by the old stagecoach road. "There's the cabin where we'll film more scenes for *Skystone Canyon*."

Barrett glanced up at the cloudless sky above them, taking in its infinite blue.

"Do you know why they call that spot Skystone Canyon?" he asked.

"Well, Mister Know-It-All," Lainey replied with a self-satisfied smirk. "This time I *do* happen to know a thing or two about the area, since I researched it for my role." She nodded at the tight box canyon below, sandwiched between cliffs and ribboned at the bottom by a meandering river. "My character Ada Holdwell is in quite a fix," she explained. "Her life is stuck like that log cabin down there, and she has to fight alone against the elements, cattle rustlers, dirty-dealing ranchers— you name it. But no matter how trapped she feels, she can always look up at the sky and allow it to remind her of hope. There's even a line in the movie: As long as the open sky remains, the soul can roam free."

Barrett couldn't keep his gaze off the pure blue of Lainey's wistful eyes, and he seemed to be comparing their color to the sky above them. "A long time ago," he pointed out, "turquoise was found by that river. A thin vein was exposed by natural erosion, and my mother said her people went down there and collected it for sacred purposes."

A faraway look came to Lainey's eyes, as though she were reaching into her mind for a hint of memory. "Your mom, she came to the horse camp a few times," she said, nodding slowly. "I remember her—she was very beautiful. And she looked, you know…"

"Apache?" replied Barrett. He raised his chin with pride. "She grew up on the Jicarilla reservation in Dulce. Her ancestors were a horse tribe. That's why she always came to the camp to see how I was doing. It meant everything to her for me to understand the spirit of the horses, and to know about the turquoise…."

His voice trailed off.

"The turquoise?" she said. "I guess I'm not seeing the connection—"

"Horses and turquoise were the Apache's protection," he explained. "In war, the courage and pure hearts of the horses —and the power of turquoise—kept my mother's people safe. Those sacred stones," he gazed down into the canyon, "were attached to arrows to make a warrior's aim straight and used as amulets to ward off evil. The Zuni called turquoise the fallen sky stone that was hidden deep in Mother Earth, and it was considered more precious than gold. My mother's ancestors called it *dáatł'iiji* and revered it for the same reason. She used to tell me as long as you had turquoise with you, you were never trapped. You'd always find a way. My ancestor Iron Feather may not have left his descendants much, but he did hand down his medicine pouch that included his sacred turquoise stones."

Lainey gazed into the canyon as well, studying the vibrant blue reflected on the river from the sky above. After appreciating the beauty of the site, a slight smile came to her lips. "Don't you think it's a little ironic, Barrett, that your ancestor was a famous outlaw, and now *you're* a police officer?"

"Not at all," Barrett replied. "We've both devoted our lives to justice."

"Justice? Where's the justice in robbing stagecoaches and trains?"

Barrett glared at Lainey. "Obviously, you didn't hear the whole story," he pointed out. "Iron Feather never kept a dime for himself. He used the money to fund his tracking missions."

"Missions?"

His trips to find children from the Native American families he was close to who'd been sent against their will to boarding schools around the country. He kidnapped them and brought them back. To his way of thinking," Barrett's voice became low and serious, "the government's policy of forcing children from their homes was an act of war. And Iron Feather fully intended to win."

Tears welled in the corners of Lainey's eyes, and her throat choked up a little. It was true—she'd never heard that part of the story, only the legends about the Bandits Hollow Gang's outlaw exploits. She didn't know Barrett's ancestor had his own ideas about achieving "justice."

"Speaking of justice," Barrett said, staring at Lainey while he pulled out a ziplock bag from his back jeans pocket, "I should tell you the real reason I wanted to get you alone this evening." He held up the zip log bag that contained a piece of brown leather. "When I stopped your wagon team during our action scene today, one of the horses' harnesses fell right off in my hand. This piece from the headstall connecting the leather to the bit appears to have been sliced in two. The leather looks brand new, Lainey—there's no reason it would have torn."

Lainey heaved a sigh. "So now you're a detective, too? Just think, all this time I believed the con that you wanted to go out with me! When are you ever *not* working, Barrett Iron Feather?"

"Now."

Barrett seized Lainey by the shoulders and stole a reckless kiss. His lips melded against hers with a force that left her completely broadsided. Nevertheless, Lainey couldn't stop herself from falling into the sensual taste of his mouth as his lips worked over hers. He clutched the back of her neck to pull her in even closer. Her body felt as if it had been ignited by a fire, and despite attempting to brace herself, she fell limp under his grip. This is pure heaven, high on a windswept ridge, Lainey thought as heat rippled throughout her body, making her feel like her vertebra might melt. Gasping, the two of them finally broke apart, when Barrett's searing gaze met hers.

"I hope that settles once and for all whether I wanted to be here with you," he stated in a deep tone that made her tremble. "And quite frankly," his jaw muscles sliced back and forth in restraint, "that's not the only thing I'd like to do with you right now. But first things first: Bandits Hollow has a small police station. Between me and the Police Chief and a few other officers, we have to handle everything—including detective duty. So no matter how much I'd enjoy finding a soft place in the forest right now to kiss every inch of you, I have to face some very serious facts. First, your horse ran away with a bur under its saddle while *Skystone Canyon* was filming. Second, there was no gas in the ATVs for the crew to help you. And now this?"

He held up the ziplock bag with the piece of harness leather again.

Annoyed and desperately wishing they could have kissed for a whole lot longer, Lainey playfully tipped down Barrett's black cowboy hat until it smacked his nose.

"It's called a *low-budget* film, Sherlock. As you know, we can't even afford better stunt people, much less high-quality prop control. That harness was probably left over from some other film, or rented from a different studio. I can assure you no one checked every piece of leather prior to our scene. These are *accidents*, Barrett. You want perfection, call Steven Spielberg and DreamWorks Pictures."

Barrett arched a cynical brow, hardly convinced.

"Look," Lainey continued, "the bur was probably a random fluke. And who knows, the assistant director who was loyal to Easton could have sliced the harness with a steak knife before he took off. Grudges and power plays are rampant in the movie industry. You can't get too worked up about stuff like this on low-budget films or you'll never finish the project. Besides, I can't believe you carry around ziplock bags! Do you really think the whole world is constantly full of suspects? You call *me* serious. Look at yourself in the mirror, Barrett."

Barrett stubbornly ignored her, but she could tell from the narrow squint of his gaze that her comments had gotten under his skin. "For your information, Miss Neil," he said as he replaced the ziplock bag into his pocket, "I'm the chief security officer for *Skystone Canyon* until it finishes, which makes me head detective as well. So no matter how sassy you get about it, I *will* do everything in my power to keep you safe. Got that? Which means *never* dismissing evidence, even if it doesn't fit into your logic. "

Lainey's heart raced at the smoldering seriousness behind his big, dark eyes, but she folded her arms to put up a tough front anyway. "Has anybody told you lately that you're impossible, Officer Iron Feather?" she retorted. "For crying out loud, this is supposed to be a dinner date, and so far in between one kiss and your paranoid conspiracy theories, I've only gotten hungrier by the second." She gazed down at a vast, green valley to the west of the ridge with several ranch houses and corrals, watching a curl of smoke rise in the distance. "Please tell me that's your cookout going on down there," she pleaded, pointing at the fire. "Because the last time I checked, you owe me a dinner. And at this point, I'm starving."

12

B arrett and Lainey headed down the mountain toward the large ranch with the campfire smoke in the valley below. When they finally reached a dirt road, *Hayiitka* lifted up his nose and nickered, as if he expected dinner soon as well. He tugged impatiently on the bit, and soon Lainey spotted a large timber frame over an entrance road to the ranch. Hanging from the top was a sign with the words *Iron Feather Brothers Ranch* branded into the wood.

Lainey pulled back on the reins, stopping for moment to take in the massive main house that was the size of a luxury hotel, adorned with timber and stone accents and winged on either side by elegant guesthouses. A short distance away were two lofty barns and several corrals filled with horses, cattle, and even buffalo. The green pastures that stretched beyond the architecturally stunning buildings went on for miles.

"H-Hold on a minute," Lainey stuttered, pointing at the

wooden ranch sign. "That's *your* last name." Dumbstruck, she gazed at the expansive property with her mouth slung open. Sure, she'd seen her share of fancy estates at cocktail parties owned by Hollywood mogul types—but this enormous spread put their idea of opulent real estate to shame.

"Barrett," she said, turning toward him in her saddle, "when I met you at horse camp, I sort of got the impression that, um….you know, you and your family were rather…"

"Poor?" Barrett smirked a little. "Damn straight we were. You probably noticed that I wore the same clothes for two whole weeks."

Lainey glanced down at her saddle. "I had a crush on a boy there my age, remember?" she confessed, fiddling with her reins. "Your clothing was the last thing on my mind."

"Really?" Barrett replied mischievously. "Because I thought a *lot* about your clothing back then. Especially the idea of removing every thread." A twinkle sparked in his eyes at the way he'd made Lainey blush. "But don't get any fancy ideas about the Iron Feather brothers based on this ranch," he warned. "It's true, Dillon and Lander and I worked our asses off to rise from poverty, and we did pretty damn good with cattle ranching and investments, among other things. But even though Lander persuaded us to build an airplane runway for the queen, to this day my brothers aren't exactly highbrow."

"The queen?" Lainey gasped. "As in…from England?"

"She happens to be a really nice lady, more down to earth than you'd suspect. She loves nothing more than spending all day on horseback with a bunch of dogs," Barrett added. "But it's all I can do to make Dillon take a bath before she comes. That's the Iron Feather brothers for you. You can take the outlaw out of the wilderness, but you can't take the wilderness out of the outlaw. At any rate, I touch base with my brothers here once a week for a cookout to go over business. Just be prepared—in spite of what you see here," he gazed out over the magnificent ranch, "Dillon and Lander can be a little rough around the edges."

Lainey meant to urge her horse forward, but she was still too stunned by all this new information. The Iron Feather brothers must be multi-millionaires, she thought. Her heart began to beat faster, unsure of what to make of such a strange turn of events in the life of her first, secret crush. She gazed at Barrett with new eyes, noticing that despite all the apparent affluence, he still seemed as hard as steel. "Barrett," she blurted, "with assets like this, you hardly need to work as a police officer anymore—"

"Oh yeah I do," Barrett cut in. He withheld a slight smile, as if amused by her naivety. "My brothers wouldn't let me quit my job if my life depended on it. If I weren't busting criminals, I'd be busting them. We were born fighters, Lainey, though the blood bond runs deep. At least police work keeps me out of trouble—especially with Dillon and Lander. Speak of the devils—"

He pointed to a tall man with long blonde hair standing near the campfire waving at them. Beside him was an even taller man with equally long hair the color of charcoal, his face as still as granite. Lainey swallowed hard. She'd never met Barrett's brothers before, and they were each physically intimidating and drop-dead gorgeous in their own way. What would they think of some B-movie actress who'd wandered onto their spread? Before she could brood on that thought,

Barrett urged his horse to break into a gallop, and she followed after him, descending down a hill to the ranch.

This time, however, she wasn't about to allow *Hayiitka* to be left in the dust.

With spitfire in her eyes, Lainey leaned forward and gave her horse full rein, staying out of lariat range from Barrett. *Hayiitka* charged forward in a fury, pounding his hooves as they raced to reach the campfire within a matter of seconds. Dillon and Lander's eyes grew wide, as if they thought she might run them over, but Lainey merely smiled and leaned way back in her saddle, pulling on the reins to bring *Hayiitka* to sliding stop, the way Barrett had shown her once with Sand when she was fourteen. Clouds of dust billowed over the campfire, mingling with the smoke, making Barrett's brothers disappear.

All Lainey could hear as Barrett and his horse arrived breathlessly behind her was coughing.

Soon, the two long-haired cowboys came back into view.

"Well I'll be damned!" cried the blonde brother. "It's about time one of the Iron Feather brothers brought home a woman who could hold her own around here!" His charming grin stretched from ear to ear. "Who do we have the pleasure of meeting here this evening, Barrett? By the way, she's way too beautiful for you."

Waving aside the dust, Barrett rolled his eyes at his brother and cleared his throat. "Lainey, meet my brother Lander." He nodded and turned his attention to the tallest brother with long, dark hair and intense, brown eyes. "And this is Dillon."

Despite Lander's effusiveness, Dillon merely nodded at Lainey. His face was as grave as an Apache warrior's, making Lainey fidget nervously in her saddle.

"I'd like to say Dillon doesn't bite," Barrett added, "but that would be a lie. If you don't set him off, you'll probably be okay—"

"Don't either of you know how to be a proper gentleman?" interrupted Lander. He bent down to a cooler on the ground and pulled out what appeared to be a homebrewed bottle of beer without a label. Popping off the cap on a rock, he poured it into a tin camp mug and held it up to her. "Come on down off that horse!" he barked, setting the mug down on a nearby log. "Dinner should be ready any minute."

Lainey descended from *Hayiitka*, only to see Dillon come up and quietly grab the reins. The horse began to rub her shoulder for a pat, which she readily provided. Then she scratched behind his ears.

"He likes you," Dillon mentioned in a gruff tone. "That's good. He doesn't like many people."

"A lot like you, bro," Barrett ribbed him.

Barrett got off his horse as well, and he and his brother walked the two mounts over to a hitching post. When they returned, Lander used a mitt to open a cast-iron Dutch oven on the campfire, giving it a stir with a metal spoon.

"Ready for elk chili?"

Lainey nearly drooled at the sight of the sumptuous-smelling dish with four golden biscuits baking on top. She nodded greedily, and Lander proceeded to fill four metal bowls for everyone and pass them around. As they dug in, he opened up his cooler again. "What's your pleasure?" he said, passing the mug of beer over to Lainey. "We've got handcrafted beer and whiskey from our very own still."

"I'll pass," replied Barrett. He shot a glance at Lainey. "I may not look like it, but I'm actually still on duty."

Lainey sighed. "Just a sip of beer, Officer Iron Feather?" she teased, holding out her mug. "It's not like you have to do security right now. We're nowhere near they *Skystone Canyon* movie set."

"You're here for a film?" pressed Dillon, narrowing his eyes to dark beads. He boldly looked Lainey up and down, then scrutinized her face as though she were one of Barrett's suspects. "Are you...Lainey Neil...the *actress?*"

"Um, yeah," Lainey replied, feeling self-conscious. She was surprised Dillon had ever heard of her, since the film project didn't have the kind of budget or A-list actors to be talked about in the media.

To her astonishment, Dillon walked right up to her and peered into her eyes. With the last glimmer of sunset on her face, her eyes appeared a rich, vivid blue.

"Sky stone," Dillon nodded. Without another word, he pulled a turquoise-colored suede pouch from his pocket, unraveling the leather tie at the top. He removed a small stone from inside and held it up to her face, explaining nothing. Lainey couldn't help noticing the stone matched her eyes.

At that moment, a great horned owl called from deep within the woods nearby. Goosebumps alighted on Lainey's skin, and she shot a glance at Barrett.

"Wait a minute," Lander broke in abruptly, squinting at Lainey. "Aren't you the girl Barrett kissed when he was fourteen? The one he's never stopped talking about?" Lander chuckled for a moment. "Your pictures were all over his room when he was a teenager at the Wilson Ranch for

Wayward Boys! He had that big poster of you from *Horse Feathers*."

"Lip it, Lander," Barrett commanded with his fists clenched, as though a deeply-guarded secret had been revealed. "I wasn't the only one at the Wilson Ranch who had a crush. Last time I checked, you're kind of stuck on Taylor Swift."

"That was only in her country phase!" Lander spit out, taking a step forward and staring Barrett down like he might deck him.

"Calm down and pour yourself some goddamn whiskey, Lander," Barrett sighed, turning to Lainey. "As you can see, it's not an Iron Feather brother get together if there ain't a fight," he smirked. "There's a reason not many women attend our cookouts."

"To be honest, I don't quite understand," Lainey mentioned hesitantly. "You and your brothers didn't remain at *home* during high school?"

"Our parents passed away in a car crash when we were in our teens," Lander explained. "After that, we didn't tend to abide by the law much—if at all."

"Half breeds weren't exactly embraced at reform school," Dillon added cryptically, rubbing his knuckles. "We earned a reputation for defending ourselves."

All at once, Lainey understood the hardened defiance she'd often caught in Barrett's eyes, ever since she'd met up with him again in Bandits Hollow. It was from...

Pain.

Loss.

And a gut-wrenching determination to survive.

No wonder he had that way of always remaining vigilant, she thought. He knew what it was like to have the people you loved most be taken away—and then be persecuted. The fact that he'd done something constructive with this life anyway, becoming a police officer and building up this ranch to its current state, was more than enough to earn her respect.

And what about her?

After all these years, she still remained a B-list actress, struggling with the ghost of her father to try and find her own way.

Barrett must have noticed the introspection in her eyes, because he took a step closer to her and handed her a warm, golden biscuit.

"You know," he said, swallowing a mouthful of chili, "telling powerful stories about courage is important. Nothing's ever been handed to you, Lainey. It takes guts to do *Skystone Canyon*, when there are probably a dozen projects with bigger paychecks."

Lainey wanted to set her chili bowl down on the ground and hug him, but that would probably embarrass him in front of his brothers. "Thanks," she simply said, feeling conflicted. Why did he go to the trouble of flirting with her on their ride, and complimenting her just now, when he'd never written her during all those years? Like a fool, she'd written him dozens of letters, within nothing in return. Even when she found out that the Wings Channel had chosen Bandits Hollow as a location, she sent one more missive in a gesture of raw hope. And what had she gotten back?

Nothing.

Lainey shrugged off the sting of disappointment. Perhaps

it was best not to read too much into any of the Iron Feather brothers. They'd had tough lives, and heaven knows, some men only like to toy with women to feed their own bruised egos.

"This chili is delicious," she said, glancing at Dillon and Lander. Her gaze drifted back to Barrett. "But the stars are starting to come out—do you have a magic trick for helping the horses find Bandits Hollow in the dark?"

"Yep," butted in Lander. "It's called our Hummer. You can board the horses here tonight, and I'll have James trailer them back to town in the morning. Sound like a plan, bro?"

Barrett shifted his gaze to Lainey. "He wouldn't be nearly so generous if he weren't trying to impress you," he mentioned with an arched brow. "If it were just me, he'd say your ancestor was an expert tracker—go find your way to Bandits Hollow in the moonlight by your own damn self."

Lander chuckled and even Dillon smirked at Barrett's words, knowing it was true.

"Well, we wouldn't want this beautiful creature to get lost, now would we?" Lander picked up a binder from the ground and handed it to Barrett. "Here's the latest stock report for our investments. Let's not bore this lovely lady with shop talk right now. After all, we want her to come back, right?"

Barrett gazed into Lainey's eyes with that same sincerity that took her breath away when she was fourteen. "Definitely," he agreed.

Despite her confused heart, Lainey felt tingles skitter up her spine and pool in her cheeks. Why did he have to be so damn contradictory? Where was he all those years?

"Are you ready to get in the Hummer?" Barrett asked,

pointing at a huge, camouflage-painted vehicle parked a few yards from the campfire. The words *Iron Feather Brothers Enterprises* were printed on the door, along with their feather-brand logo.

"Sure," Lainey replied with a sigh. "As long as we don't have to move any boulders this time."

Barrett smiled. "Well, the Hummer's built for off-roading, and it does have amazing night beam lights. But I'll go easy on you this time and take the smoother route."

❧ 13 ❧

When Barrett pulled up to the Golden Wagon Hotel later that evening, to Lainey's puzzlement, he cut the engine.

"What are you doing?" Lainey asked. "This is my stop."

"I intend to walk you to the door, Miss Neil," Barrett said. "I consider that a sign of respect."

Stunned, all Lainey could do was blush. She'd never had a man in her whole life escort her to a door, particularly in the meat-market land of Hollywood where women like her were considered a dime a dozen. Barrett's old-fashioned courtesy took her completely by surprise.

Barrett stepped out of the Hummer and walked around the other side, opening her door. Taking her by the hand, he led her up to the old stagecoach that was parked in front of the hotel, painted from top to bottom in gold. "Do you remember the time we sat in this wagon? And pretended we were on an old rerun of *Bonanza*, escaping from the bad guys?"

"Your ancestors *were* the bad guys," Lainey teased, gazing up wistfully at the stars. "You know, the stars are just as beautiful now as they were back then. I swear, you can see a million of them in Bandits Hollow."

Gently, Barrett tugged at her hand. "The only star I've ever had eyes for is you," he replied as he walked with her toward the mahogany door of the hotel. His grip felt warm and strong.

Nevertheless, Lainey whipped around. In the old-fashioned lamplight of the hotel, Barrett's chiseled features were even more handsome than she could bear, and his intense gaze was enough to make any woman swoon. She bit her lip, refusing to let his good looks sway her. "Barrett," she inhaled a deep breath and dared to broach the subject, "did you *really* have posters of me in your room at reform school?"

God as her witness, she could have sworn she a flash of crimson on Barrett's cheeks.

He stared at the sidewalk for moment, his jaw working back and forth. His grip on her hand became so tight it made her wince.

"I never got over you, Lainey," Barrett confessed, lifting his gaze to meet hers. His eyes held such raw honesty and yearning that it nearly knocked the wind out of her. Barrett stood with his lips close enough to hers that she could feel their heat. "I'm not saying you have to feel the same way," he assured her. His Adam's apple slid up and down in anticipation. It's just that...," he paused a for moment to sift through his thoughts. "My brothers were telling the truth. You've always been my dream girl."

Lainey's eyes narrowed as she did her level best to sort through her feelings of humiliation and anger, in spite of her overwhelming attraction to him right now. Gritting her teeth for a moment, she decided to let out her burning question.

"Then how come you never wrote back to me?" she asked, her voice sounding more fragile than she'd intended. Lainey yanked her hand from Barrett's, tightening her fists to try and ward off the tears that wanted to well her eyes. "Was I somehow more attractive on two-dimensional paper than in real life? I must have written to you a hundred times—"

Barrett placed both hands on either side of her shoulders against the wall of Golden Wagon Hotel, closing Lainey in and staring with a fierce longing into her eyes. For a moment, he said nothing, as if his gaze were absorbing her soul. Barrett's dark brown eyes were so riveting, Lainey thought her heart might stop.

"For your information, Miss Neil," he corrected her, "I wrote letter after letter to you, putting my heart on my sleeve for years. *Years*. Not a day has gone by that I don't think of you. And if you doubt me," he said in low tone that sent shivers down her body, "then try doubting this."

Barrett threw his cowboy hat from his head and kissed her long and slow, the kind of kiss that made her toes curl and her thoughts blur to jelly as sparks snapped up and down her spine. Then Barrett clutched her face as though he never intended to let go, kissing her so hard that Lainey could have sworn he succeeded in breathing her in. When Barrett finally released her, Lainey's eyes fluttered as if she were trying to regain consciousness.

"Why, Officer Iron Feather," she chided him, "are you allowed to behave like that on duty?"

Barrett didn't bother to smile. He simply stared into her eyes with the same ferocious intensity that sent her reeling. "As far as I'm concerned, kissing you *is* my duty." He rubbed his thumb softly over her cheek, taking in the beauty of her face under the lamplight. "I don't know why you never got my letters," he said, genuinely confused. "But I think you can tell by now that you had my heart all along."

Barrett tipped his forehead against hers. He ran his palms down her shoulders and arms to grab both her hands. Lainey felt a tremor course through his skin.

"Long ago," he confessed, "I met the most beautiful girl I'd ever seen, who showed me kindness," he gazed into her eyes, "even though she seemed a bit lost and in need of protection. But she was as brave as hell—and she told me back then that she genuinely cared about me. I guess at this point, what I want to know is…who is Lainey Neil now?"

Choked up from his words, Lainey couldn't stop the tears from forming this time. One slid down her cheek, and Barrett gently brushed it away.

"I…I think I'm still trying to find her," she replied, knowing it was probably the most honest thing she'd ever admitted in her whole life.

"Well, when you do," Barrett said, his to-die for lips rising in lop-sided smile, "do me a favor and let me know. Because I'd sure like to take her home."

Home…

After her peripatetic life, chasing one audition after the other since she'd been a teenager, there wasn't another word in the English language that meant more to Lainey Neil.

Lainey dove for another kiss with Barrett, this time slipping her hands free from his grip and linking her arms around his neck. "Maybe home isn't a place," she whispered, her voice cracking a little. "Maybe it's in my heart."

Barrett pulled back, taking in the twinkle from the streetlamp that reflected in her eyes. He lifted his finger and slowly drew a heart over her chest as though he wished with all his might that he could belong there.

Then he leaned over and pulled the brass knob on the old mahogany door to the hotel, swinging it open wide for Lainey.

"Good night, Miss Neil," Barrett whispered. "Don't forget to follow your heart. I'll see you in the morning."

14

The next day, Barrett gazed over the cattle herd in a pasture on the edge of Bandits Hollow, shaking his head. A stuntman who'd ambushed Lainey's wagon as a cattle rustler the day before had now changed clothes and was attempting to rope a Hereford while portraying one of Ada Holdwell's ranch hands during a cattle-cutting scene. To Barrett's dismay, he held his rope all wrong and failed to secure the end around the saddle horn. When he happened to get lucky and caught a cow, he was instantly yanked from his saddle and dragged to the ground.

Sand had been standing to attention with his ears perked the whole time, seemingly aware of the debacle. When Barrett gave him the cue, he bolted after the poor man being dragged like he'd been fired from a rifle. Barrett descended upon the wayward Hereford and roped him right away with the tail end tied anchored around his saddle horn. Sand planted his hooves and slid to a stop, holding the cow firm as Barrett leaped from his saddle and tied up the cow's legs to render him immobile. Then Barrett ran to the stuntman, spying the rope caught around his hand. Swiftly, he freed the man's palm from the tight coil and crouched down on his heels.

"You okay, buddy?" he asked, glancing at the torn leather on his hand. "Good thing you were wearing gloves. Next time, don't wrap a rope around your hand whenever you're near cows or horses. That's a good way to lose body parts."

"*Now* you tell me," grumbled the stuntman as he rolled onto his knees, rubbing his sore hand.

Barrett ignored him and walked over to Sand, easily manhandling the cow to release him from the rope. The cow skittered back to the herd in a woozy line as if he didn't know what hit him. Barrett dropped Sand's reins to ground tie and returned to check on the stuntman for broken bones and bruises, going over his arms and legs and nodding at the director that he'd be okay.

"Damn the Wings Channel all to hell!" cried Harper, storming up to the two men. She was wearing a black, form-fitting dress with a plunging neckline that hugged her curves so tightly she could have stopped traffic. The early morning light sparkled off her Bourbon glass, which she gripped fiercely underneath blood-red fingernails. "How *dare* the studio contract with a stunt company that has no experience working cattle? This is a *western* film!" She thrust her Bourbon glass into Barrett's hand and whipped around to face the cameramen a few yards away, making a T sign with her hands for a time out.

"*Skystone Canyon* crew!" she bellowed loud enough to wake the dead. "All of the actors and stuntmen for this scene need to line up over here this instant. Our cowboy cop is going to give you a roping lesson," she ordered, "so nobody loses any fingers and tries to sue me."

"Roping lesson, eh?" Barrett responded, raising a brow. "Listen Miss Stone," he brazenly defied her without being the least bit distracted by her Hollywood status, "you need to understand real quick that nobody can perform miracles with your actors and crew in one lesson. The best I can do is keep people from injury, which does happen to fall under my job description as a security officer. The only reason I'm doing this, or anything else for your goddamned film, is so it wraps faster and I can go back to my real job—which happens to be arresting bad guys and saving lives. And just so we're clear," he leaned into her face menacingly, giving her a frozen stare, "I *never* take orders from *you*."

Harper's eyes grew twice their size as he shoved the Bourbon glass back in her hand. "Here, throw this down before we start," Barrett demanded. "Alcohol will make the crew's roping skills look a whole lot better on film when we're done."

"Uh…gladly," Harper replied in rattled tone. She quickly straightened her back so no one would see her appear weak as her crimson lips curled in a smirk, admiring his boldness. Then she knocked back her glass of Bourbon to save her dignity, finishing it in one gulp.

"You—pioneer girl," she pointed to Lainey, who was heading toward her in front of the other actors and stuntmen. "Get over here fast and show me you can swing a rope, before we lose any more time."

Lainey sucked in deep breath with caution in her eyes. It

had been a decade since she'd handled a rope at horse camp, with no time for a practice session to ready her for filming, like she'd done with the wagon scene. Sheepishly, she stepped up to Barrett.

"Ready for a trip down memory lane?" he asked her. "We used to practice for hours roping a set of old horns attached to a hay bale. Until you finally graduated to a calf."

Lainey's face flushed. "I, um, I was pretty bad with a rope back then, wasn't I?" She twisted her hands together at the prospect. As I recall, I missed so many times, the calf got bored and laid down in the middle of the corral for a nap."

"That's okay," Barrett assured her, trying to hold back a grin. "You looked pretty cute trying to rope him."

"Even though I was a chubby teenager who was all thumbs?" Lainey sighed.

Barrett paused for a moment, his eyes tracing her fit body from head to toe in her calico dress with raw admiration. The way his gaze lingered on the edges of her curves made warmth prickle at her cheeks.

"You were *never* chubby, Lainey," he declared in a low tone. "In fact," he met her eyes with an indignant gaze that caught her unawares, making her heart do flip flops, "you've always been *perfect*."

Barrett patted her cheek before he turned and grabbed the rope from his saddle on Sand. Then he collected more ropes from the other stunt horses and returned to the group, eyeing a couple of Herefords nearby.

"Most cattle cutting is done on horseback," Barrett announced to the group, "when you want to separate a particular cow from the herd for doctoring or branding. Sand over there," he glanced back at his horse, "is so good he can practically work cattle without a rider. But for now, we'll just practice roping for a few minutes on a stationary target so you can get the feel of working the rope in your hands before we mount again." He stepped over to a folding chair by one of the cameras and dragged it out to the pasture a few yards away and set it down, motioning for the others to follow.

"Okay everybody," Barrett said after the small cluster of people had joined him, "I want each of you to take a rope, holding it at the top of the coil," he instructed as he passed out ropes. Lainey and the stuntmen did as they were told, while Cayden Hart shook his head as if he'd been sent back to sixth grade. Barrett shot him an icy stare, as though the consequences of defying his orders might include a horse whipping, and Cayden rapidly gripped his rope. "Now, feed some rope through the hondo," Barrett continued, tapping an eyelet at the end of the rope, "until you've made a big loop."

He held up his rope to demonstrate. "Once you've made nice loop and stretched about an arm's length of rope to hold in your other hand, practice swinging the loop over your head, turning your wrist upside down to complete the tail end of your swing, so you don't whack yourself in the face."

One stuntman had been too eager and already smacked himself before Barrett had finished his sentence. He rubbed his cheek vigorously and gave it another go, completing an overhead circle.

Fortunately for Lainey, the hand motion came back to her rather quickly, and her chest swelled with pride at the smooth circles she was able to make over her head.

Barrett's eyes glinted with satisfaction that his instruction years ago appeared to remain in her muscle memory. "When you're ready," he directed, "you'll need to throw this rope, using your hand and arm in the correct motion so the rope lands where you want around the horns."

Barrett stepped up to the folding chair. "Always approach the cow from the left hand side. Keep three coils in one hand as you circle your loop over your head. Then aim your rope using the far end of the loop, not the hondo, and cast the loop with your thumb forward, not your pinky finger. Throw your rope over the bottom right side of the cow's head or horn, catching the other side of the loop on the left side. Then follow through with a straight arm, as if the rope were an extension of your body, and pull the slack without letting go of the coil in your other hand. Remember, when you do this on horseback, you'll need to stand up in your stirrups—and *never* wind the tail end around your hand."

Barrett pulled several more folding chairs into the pasture, setting them a few yards apart while the cows looked on warily.

"Ready?" he called to the crew. "Come on out and start practicing."

He watched as they circled their ropes over their heads, making clumsy attempts to snare folding chairs, some forgetting to keep their arms straight and knocking the chairs over, while others managed to snag themselves in coils of rope. Lainey's first few efforts were slightly better, but her rope kept landing lopsided, and the frustration began to show on her face.

"Keep your thumb up!" Barrett reminded her, motioning

to her with his hand in the correct position. "You'll throw a lot straighter."

"Really?" Lainey replied, a wicked gleam surfacing in her eye. "Let me give that method a shot."

She whipped around and snagged Barrett with her loop, yanking her rope tight to pin his arms to his sides. "You're right!" she giggled, a bit stunned that she'd succeeded. "Works like a charm."

"Congratulations, Miss Neil," Barrett replied dryly. "Looks like you're ready to try your hand on a real calf." He glanced down at the rope cinched around his chest. "That means you need to let me go."

"I don't think you're in a position to issue orders," she challenged, making no effort to hide her laughter.

Barrett glared at Lainey, and before she could blink, he'd whipped his rope around her, pulling it as tight as a vise. "Aren't I?" he taunted with a crooked grin. "I do believe I have more experience tying up the hooves of unruly critters than you." He boldly stepped toward her as if he were about to do a demonstration.

"Kidding!" Lainey yelped, not wanting to find herself hog tied in front of the crew. She swiftly loosened her rope until it dropped from his chest to the ground. "See? You're free now!"

At that moment, a sharp, popping sound erupted from the back of the cattle herd in the pasture, followed by a deep, thundering rumble. When Lainey turned in the direction of the noise, the Herefords had already begun to charge toward the film crew, lowing in panic.

"S-Stampede!" cried a stuntman, frozen at the sight.

"Run! Everyone make a left and go back over to the set!"

Barrett commanded. "Cattle are unlikely to turn once they're in motion." Quickly, he grabbed Lainey and hoisted her in his arms, carrying her as fast as he could and setting her onto Sand. "Hold on!" he said as he slapped his horse hard on the rump to make him bolt back toward the cameras. The horse veered away from the herd, out of harm's way.

When Barrett spun around, he spied Cayden Hart standing paralyzed in front of the oncoming stampede in shock. Barrett dashed over to him and knocked him down, covering him with his body. He ripped out his concealed weapon from his hip holster and fired a couple of shots into the dirt in front of the cattle, causing the herd to curve past them like a raging, flowing river. One cow got confused and jumped over them, barely missing Barrett and Cayden with its hooves. The cattle's rampage continued to send dust roiling everywhere, obscuring the pasture from view. Dark dust clouds passed over Barrett and Cayden like a thunder storm, until the pounding hooves slowly began to ease up. Soon the dust began to settle, allowing Barrett to stand up again and look around, registering that the other actors and crew were indeed safe by the set.

"You fool!" Barrett chastised Cayden, yanking him by the elbow to his feet. "Why didn't you go over to the cameras like I told you? We could have both been *killed*—"

"Nobody prepared me for a fricking stampede when I signed the contract for this stupid film!" Cayden spewed, throwing his rope into Barrett's face. "Don't worry about me anymore, Officer Red Neck." He turned on his heels and began to stomp away from the pasture. "Because I quit!"

15

B arrett scoured the trampled ground where the cattle had grazed before they'd gotten spooked, spying a small area littered with shreds of cigarette papers alongside sawdust scattered on the grass. Meticulously, he pulled out gloves and picked up each remnant of cigarette paper, noting the tell-tale smoky color on the blast edges and twists at the tops. Placing the papers in a ziplock bag, he headed over to Lainey, who was sitting beside the other crew members eating lunch.

"Evidence," he said when he reached her, holding up his bag. "Despite what you see in western movies, it's pretty rare for a cattle herd to stampede in broad daylight. Usually that occurs at night, when stray sounds can makes them fear a predator is near. But in our case, the predator showed up in daytime."

"Predator? I'm not quite following you." Lainey replied.

She picked up a plate with one of Nell's luscious bacon-avocado burgers and homemade kettle chips from the Golden Wagon Restaurant and passed it to Barrett. Then she nodded at the bag. "What are those?"

"Pop-Its, poppers, bang snaps—little fireworks you throw on the ground to make a loud sound. A pile of them were left strategically in the pasture. All a cow had to do was step on them, and the blasts would make a stampede occur. Pretty clever."

"Wait, are you saying you think someone did this on *purpose*? Any kid could have simply dropped a few on the Fourth of July. Maybe a cow didn't step on them till now."

"True," Barrett conceded. "Except for the fact that the holiday was a month ago, and we've had summer afternoon rains since then, which would have easily dissolved these paper wrappings." He held the bag closer so she could see the crisp cigarette papers that enclosed the silver fulminate and sawdust on the poppers. "These fireworks are fresh, Lainey."

"Birthday party?" She shrugged. "You know how clumsy kids are with party favor bags. They could have dropped them, right?"

"Or this film could be Apollo 13," grumbled one of the grips from the crew. "I swear, I've never seen so many accidents on a set in the span of only a couple of days." He glanced at Barrett. "Is there some curse in Bandits Hollow we should know about?"

Deb sat across from Lainey, shaking her head. "I hate to agree," she mentioned, putting down her burger on a plate. "I've never seen anything like it." Her eyes narrowed at Lainey with a worried look. "First the director got arrested, then

Cayden Hart jumped ship. Now crazy cattle?" She leaned in closer so the other crew members wouldn't hear. "Is this movie worth your reputation, Lainey?" she said. "At this point, I don't think anyone would blame you if you backed out. Remember the boondoggle when your agent pushed you to do that horrible dating show with a live video feed on MatchCraze?"

"What's MatchCraze?" Barrett asked, observing Lainey's beet-red cheeks.

"Oh God, it's this awful internet dating site," Lainey replied, wishing she could crawl into a hole and hide. Deb was right—the brief, reality-show experience had been a terrible career move after her series *Horse Feathers* had ended, during a time when she was vulnerable and wanted to prove to audiences that she was an adult. Her agent had convinced her the gig would bring her great "exposure," but all she got was a bunch of leering, wannabe actors who were far to eager to shove their tongues down her throat to get a close-up on camera. "Believe me," Lainey sighed, "it's no fun trying to transition from child actor to adult roles."

"It ain't exactly a picnic for the rest of us either, sister," snapped one of the cameraman as he walked by with his lunch. He shot a glance at Harper Stone, who was refilling her glass of Bourbon and downing another shot. "I'm surprised Harper hasn't given up the ghost by now on this dog of a project," the man complained as he shook his head and walked away.

Lainey's hands balled into fists, her eyes burning. "*Skystone Canyon* isn't a dog," she hissed, shooting a glance at Deb and Barrett. "As a matter of fact, my agent didn't want me to do this film. I chose it because of the character of Ada Holdwell, who *never* gives up. And I'm not about to give up, either—no matter how flaky some of the other people on this project are."

Barrett finished chewing a bite of his burger and crouched down, meeting Lainey's gaze. "Then are you going to take that?" He nodded at the snarky cameraman. "Or are you going to bust your ass to rescue this film?"

To Lainey's astonishment, he set down his plate and locked his large hands on her shoulders, staring her in the eye. "Do you remember, once upon a time, how I made you promise never to let anyone abuse you again?"

A shiver rippled through Lainey's shoulders at his question.

"H-How could I forget," she stammered. "That day changed my life."

"Well, *now* is one of those times, Lainey. Unlike the crew, or even Cayden Hart, you're the one who has everything to lose here. It's *your* reputation that's on the line—whether you can be a viable adult actress who's taken seriously, or just another wannabe who bungled her last shot. How much does this movie cost, anyway?"

"Um, about…a million," Lainey replied, biting back the sting of being confronted by Barrett, even though she knew he was telling the truth. "Like I said, it's low budget."

Barrett arched a brow. "Low budget or not," he said sternly, "the Wings Channel is going to notice if they wasted a million bucks on you. Either because the film never got finished, or it became a laughing stock. The crew will just get other jobs—they're probably union, anyway. But if you let this film fail, Lainey, everyone will blame you…and Harper."

"How do you know?" Lainey implored. "You're not in the film business—"

Barrett stared at her with such a hard gaze that her words evaporated before she could finish. "Because they always blame the women," he said with a surprising amount of venom. "My mother was full-blood Apache, Lainey. Anything we did out of order at the Wilson Ranch for Wayward Boys, the school director blamed her. And loudly, I might add. He ran around saying we have bad blood, defiant blood. And the truth is—we DO. Because our mother taught us to never back down to *anybody*."

Barrett released her, and Lainey stared at his large knuckles littered with scars, the same ones that had decked her own father once. Though she tried to will it away, her mouth curled up a little as she peered into his eyes.

"I always knew you were a badass," Lainey remarked.

"So are *you*," Barrett added, in all seriousness. He held up his ragged knuckles to hers, noticing their scars matched. "Now, when are you going to decide to fight for this film?"

Lainey shifted her attention to Harper, who was walking past them and carrying a glass of Bourbon in a wobbly line back to her trailer, without even bothering to grab lunch. Lainey chewed on her lip for a moment.

"Right now," she asserted to Barrett with determination in her eyes. She set aside her half-eaten burger on a plate and inhaled a deep breath, standing up from her folding chair. "I'm going to go talk to Harper right now."

16

L ainey's hand trembled on the door handle to the trailer. She'd knocked and called out a few times, but Harper hadn't bothered to answer. Even more unnerving was the fact that she'd overheard two crew members as they crossed the equipment area trying to decide whether they should quit soon or get stuck with the bad reputation of a film that was doomed to "flop." Sucking up her courage, Lainey knocked once more, then boldly turned the handle anyway and gave the door a yank.

Inside the trailer was Harper, seated at a small table with her head in her hands beside her usual glass of Bourbon.

Lainey cleared her throat to announce her presence, but Harper didn't look up.

"M-Ms. Stone?" she stumbled over her words. "We need to talk."

Harper glanced up with red-stained eyes. "If you're gonna

quit this film like the other losers," she growled, "then for God's sake, get the hell out of my face and don't ever darken my door again. While you're at it, you can kiss your paychecks for the last two weeks goodbye."

"I'm *not* leaving," Lainey spit back. Heart drumming, she stepped into the trailer without invitation and sat down across from Harper, leveling her gaze. "That's what I came here to tell you. I want us to go forward with this film—Cayden or no Cayden," she said through gritted teeth.

Harper narrowed her eyes. "Good riddance to that pretty-boy asshole," she grumbled, waving her hand dismissively in the air. She shook her head and reached for her glass of Bourbon, only to have Lainey brazenly seize it from her grip. She set it down on the table out of Harper's grasp.

For the first time since Lainey had met the Hollywood icon, she caught the petrified look in her eyes, the slight tremble of her fingers that gripped the edge of the table a little too tightly. The sight of this ice queen suddenly appearing so vulnerable shook Lainey to her core.

It was no secret that Harper was scared to death—

Because she had everything to lose, too.

"Look," Lainey met her gaze head on, "me—you—we have far too much at stake to abandon this project now. No matter how you slice it, we both know we're the ones who'll take the hit if it's anything less than a success. The people who'll lose their careers over the fate of *Skystone Canyon* are sitting right here in this cheap-ass trailer."

"Why the hell do you think I'm drowning my liver?" Harper snapped bitterly. "*I'm* the one who pushed the Wings Channel to option the script and finance the whole damn thing. They'll carry me out the door in a casket faster than you can say movie disaster."

Lainey nodded slowly. "Well, if it's any consolation, I'll be six-feet under right beside you," she replied in a matter-of-fact tone. "With a headstone that reads *Another former child star who bit the dust and blew her big chance*. Do they happen to have any two-for-one deals for funerals in Hollywood?"

Harper's crimson lips tugged into a smile. "Aw, honey, they'll just dump us in the same grave and call it a wash."

Lainey reached out and grabbed Harper's hand, gripping it tightly. "Listen, Ms. Stone," she said, "you're one of the most beautiful and talented people I've ever seen, in everything you've done. And they way you took control of this film— you're a total badass."

"Then why the hell am I shaking in my boots, pioneer girl?"

"Because what we're doing is breaking the mold—on our own terms. A movie about a tough woman who prevails against the odds? Look around you in Hollywood. Who else has the guts to make this film? I, for one, am not about to let it go down the drain."

Lainey got up from her seat and picked up Harper's glass of Bourbon, turning to pour it in the trailer sink. "The only thing that needs to go down the drain is your crutch," she insisted, opening the cupboards overhead to locate more liquor. Lainey filled her arms with bottles and yanked opened the door of the trailer, tossing each one outside with a crash. Then she whipped around and glared at Harper.

"Cayden's gone. Easton's gone. One of the cameramen's gone. And near as I can tell, so are a couple of grips. Fess up right now, Ms. Stone, before I waste another second of my good faith and time. Are you in, or are you out?"

Harper paused and stared at the chipped formica on the trailer table, stained with far too many rings from coffee and Bourbon glasses. She cleared her throat.

"Well, we can keep the footage we already have of Cayden and use that cowboy cop whenever we need a shot from behind—they have the same dark hair color. And the cameras are digital. I'm sure a couple of second-string cameramen would love to step up to the plate to beef up their resumes. If we have to, we can finish this."

"That's not good enough," Lainey challenged her, "and you know it." She slapped her hands down on the trailer table and glared at Harper. "I repeat: Are you *in*, or are you *out?*"

In spite of Lainey's gutsiness, she feared what she might really see in Harper's eyes. Maybe her haughty demeanor had simply been bluster, and Harper was like all of the other weak Hollywood players she'd known through the years who'd dump their own mothers in a ditch if they thought it would salvage their reputations. Yet curiously, Lainey thought she spied a fire beginning to smolder in Harper's eyes.

In silence, Harper slipped on her mile-high black heels and straightened her back, slowly rising to her feet. Then she stepped over to Lainey and carefully placed her hand on her cheek, giving her a pat and peering into her eyes.

She didn't say another word.

It didn't matter, because Lainey could feel the iron will behind her gaze.

Harper quietly dug into her pocket and pulled out her large, black sunglasses, slipping them on her face to cover her blood-shot eyes. Then she threw open the door of her trailer with a loud thwack and stood with her hands on her hips in the doorway like a boss. The sun reflected in a corona of light off her pale hair, giving an otherworldly glow to her goddess features. The sight gave Lainey goosebumps.

"*Skystone Canyon* crew!" she announced at the top of her lungs, listening to her words echo across the film equipment area. "It's time to do or die! Whoever's ready to create a movie that will shake the hell out of Tinsel Town and make audiences want to stand up and cheer, get your asses over here for instructions about tomorrow's filming. The rest of you can kindly…go…fuck…yourselves." She glanced down at the broken Bourbon bottles laying on the grass in front of her, reflecting fractured glints of sunlight. Drawing a deep breath, she left the doorway and headed for the refrigerator inside the trailer, opening it up and pulling out two slices of red velvet cake.

"If I've learned anything in Hollywood," Harper said, handing Lainey a piece of cake, "it's that courage isn't the absence of fear." She downed a huge bite and brushed the crumbs from her lips, nodding at Lainey to do the same. "From now on, you and I eat adventure for breakfast. Got that, pioneer girl? Now let's go make this goddamned film great."

❧ 17 ❧

O nce Harper gave her pep talk for the next day's filming to the remaining crew, she spent a few hours going over the dailies with the film editors and then announced to everyone that she was taking them to the Outlaw's Hideout Bar and Grill in Bandits Hollow that evening to thank them for their loyalty to *Skystone Canyon*. Lainey couldn't help giving her a high-five afterwards and exclaiming "Way to go, Boss!" before she turned to head off the set. Meandering her way around the cameras and film equipment, she spied a long, dark shadow on the grass that made her glance up.

There was Barrett, standing with his large arms folded.

"I'm proud of you," he said in a genuine tone.

"You…are?" Lainey replied. "For what?"

"For having the guts to confront Harper. I always knew you had grit."

Lainey's eyes narrowed. "What do you mean? Did you *listen in* on our conversation?"

"It's my job," Barrett replied. "I keep people safe."

"There's nothing dangerous about talking to the head of my film!" Lainey asserted.

"There is if she takes a swing at you," Barrett pointed out. "Especially after the kinds of things you said to her that she probably didn't want to hear. Not to mention having the guts to break all of her alcohol bottles. Intoxicated people can be extremely volatile—believe me, I know. And from what I can tell, Harper's usually drunk off her ass."

Lainey bit back a giggle. "Yeah, guess you're on target with that one."

"Besides," Barrett unfolded his arms and moved closer, "can't you take a damn compliment for once?" He winked, linking his arm in hers. "C'mon, Miss Bravery, let's head over to the Outlaw's Hideout Bar and Grill. The bill's on Harper, and I think the crew needs to see your confidence in her."

"Hold on!" called out Deb, lugging her makeup case beside her while Lainey and Barrett stepped onto Main Street. "You haven't removed your makeup properly yet, Missy," she chided Lainey. "You don't want to break out before filming ends, do you? Remember when that happened on *Horse Feathers*? Movie makeup sure clogs pores."

Lainey heaved a sigh and glanced at Barrett. "I hate to say it, but Deb's right," she admitted grudgingly. "My face was a mess that time. We practically had to use spackling the next day to cover the blemishes."

"Luckily, your skin looks perfect au naturel," Barrett said with a twinkle in his eye. The way his gaze ran over her body, hesitating on each curve, made heat surface on Lainey's cheeks, as if he were wondering how the rest of her looked naked as well.

Deb ignored him and applied a thick cream with her fingers to strip Lainey's face of makeup, then dabbed on astringent with a ball of cotton. "There," she said cheerfully, gazing at Lainey's face with pride, "now your pores will be happy. Ready to go to the bar?" She tucked her cosmetic removers into her makeup case and closed it with a snap before slipping her hand into her pocket. Then she lifted up a mobile phone. "Oh crumbs, I forgot—here's your cell that you asked me to hold for you during roping practice. I think your agent might have called today."

Lainey winced. After the last contract he'd mailed her about the Vegas gig that she'd dismissed, she wondered if he wanted to keep pressuring her into that god-awful job. Still, he was her agent, and returning his call was a professional courtesy. "Guess I'd better bite the bullet and do this," she said to Deb, steeling herself for her agent's silver tongue. She hit the speed dial on her phone. "This should only take a minute," she promised Barrett.

"Ron?" she asked as soon as he picked up. "Hi there, this is Lainey. You called earlier? Please don't tell me you're going to try to sell me Vegas again—"

"No, no!" he replied in a loud burst of enthusiasm. "I've got something *much* better. You won't believe this—there's a TV studio in New York that's paying big bucks right now for former child stars to appear in their new show, *Where Are They Now?* Before you say no, Lainey, I want you to hear me out. They've swung a slick deal to broadcast it on cable. There's a ton of money behind it, and it doesn't matter how fat or drugged out the actor is—the bigger the mess, the better!"

"This is supposed to be a *comedy*?" Lainey said, floored. "Sounds more like a tragedy—"

"Yes!" Ron cut her off. "It's a comedy full of slapstick, one-liners, and pratfalls. Kind of like a mixture between *Saturday Night Live* and *The Brady Bunch* goes to rehab, if you know what I mean."

"No, I don't know what you mean," Lainey replied flatly. "This project sounds humiliating."

"Look," Ron continued in a serious tone, "you're not getting any younger, Lainey. And you're way beyond the gravy days of your popular Q rating in Hollywood. People age, Lainey, and sometimes life knocks them down. This show has a real talent for making people appear entertaining and allowing audiences to connect with their favorite old stars. Besides, you could stand to loosen up for a change—you've been so serious lately! And the best part is you get to make bank."

Lainey's eyes narrowed. "And so do *you*, Ron. By peddling the misery of washed up child actors?"

Deb tapped Lainey on the shoulder. "Hold on a sec," Lainey told Ron.

"If this is about another project after *Skystone Canyon*," Deb encouraged her, "you might at least think about for a couple of days. You don't have anything lined up after the movie. And with the way your dad gutted your finances, maybe it will give you a cushion?"

Lainey paused to mull it over for a moment, when she saw Barrett shoot her a fierce look. To her surprise, he grasped her by the elbow and pulled her aside.

"Listen, Lainey," he said, "it's obvious this Ron guy is pressuring you. And from the look in your eyes, it's something you don't want to do. So I have one question for you: Doesn't Ron work for *you*? Like your father once did?"

Taken aback by his vehemence, Lainey shrugged. "Yeah… he does," she replied hesitantly, unsure of where this was going.

"Then don't you see a pattern here?" Barrett pressed. "Why do you care about pleasing any of these people? They should be jumping hoops for *you*. You're the boss, Lainey—like Harper."

"I-I know, but it's just that, I'm afraid projects will dry up if I don't take something Ron offers once in a while—"

"Lainey," Barrett interrupted her, shaking his head, "all the money in the world won't make you happy if you're not doing what you really want to do. "

"You're one to talk!" Lainey fired back. "You're *rich*! You can afford to think this way."

"We weren't wealthy when we started. Of all people, you should know that, since you met me when I was a teen," he declared. "After my parents died we had nothing. My brothers and I built everything from the ground up."

"Out of anger?" she insisted, noticing the vehemence hadn't left his face.

"That's better than caving in all the time," Barrett shot back.

As much as he'd gotten her hackles up, Lainey couldn't manage to get the image of the frayed clothes he used to wear at camp out of her mind, always toting around a century-old saddle and a threadbare Navajo blanket. She knew perfectly well his parents were poor. Searching the ground at her feet, a twinge of remorse stung her heart.

"You and your brothers fought to be where you are, didn't you?" she said, her voice softened.

Barrett remained silent for a moment. Then he cleared his throat. "We were at rock bottom, Lainey. So we made a choice to do the things we love, because we had nothing left to lose. Sure, me and my brothers were angry as hell, but we also had big ideas. Big dreams. It's pretty obvious I don't *have* to be a police officer. But I *want* to make the world a safer place." He gently lifted a strand of her hair and curled it behind her ear. "For people like *you*."

Lainey took in a deep breath, strengthened by his words and bracing herself to tell Ron no about the New York gig. But when she returned the cell phone to her ear, she got a dial tone.

Ron had hung up—

"He's gone," she shrugged as she hit speed dial again, collecting her thoughts regarding what to say to him. "Ron," she said when he picked up, "listen, about the New York TV show, I think you and I both know that the whole point is to showcase child stars whose lives have become train wrecks. To make them look as trashy and pathetic as possible."

"Pathetic is the point!" Ron retorted. "The worse you are, the more audiences will love it! It'll be like printing money! I hate to tell you this, Lainey, but I heard about Easton Wolfe getting arrested and Cayden Hart walking off the *Skystone Canyon* set. How much more evidence do you need that this movie is taking a nose dive? At least the New York project will bolster your bank account for a while and add comedy to your resume. By the way, they want you to audition next week wearing that cute little outfit you used to wear on *Horse Feathers.*"

Lainey's eyes widened in shock. "So I can look like an adult still pretending to be teenager? That's ridiculous! The answer is a firm no, Ron. I mean it—you need to find me better parts."

"Come on, Lainey," Ron whined, "you're being oversensitive. Wouldn't a big fat check make you feel better now?"

"I *mean it*, Ron," Lainey insisted. "You need to find me meatier roles." She glanced up at Barrett for support. "Adult parts with integrity and…grit."

"I don't know what's gotten into you. You're not at all the girl I met as a teen who I turned into a star. If you're not going to take the comedy gig, all I have to say to you, Lainey Neil, is…we're through."

"Through?" she said, puzzled.

The only sound on the other end was a dial tone that rang as loudly as a death knell.

Lainey's mouth dropped in shock. She held up the phone so Barrett could hear, unable to believe her ears.

18

L ainey's face was lit up a furious scarlet from the glow of the neon sign at the Outlaw's Hideout Bar and Grill depicting a bandit firing his six-shooter. She stood on the wooden boardwalk outside the bar with her hands balled into fists, gulping a few breaths in an effort to calm down.

It didn't work.

She shot a glance at Barrett beside her.

"I-I simply can't bring myself to go in the bar just yet," she stammered, on the verge of hyperventilating. "How can I bring myself to have *fun* right now, when Ron just trashed our agent-client agreement? All because he doesn't want to get off his butt and search for better roles!" Her indignant gaze met Barrett's dark brown eyes. "Do you have any *idea* how much money I've made him over the years? He's been my agent since I was a teen!"

Barrett nodded sympathetically. For a moment, he opened the door and disappeared inside the bar to bring back a red and white paper bag from the popcorn machine. He held it out to Lainey.

Lainey yanked it from his hand and began huffing into the bag, blowing the paper in and out like a balloon until she managed to calm her nerves. When her breathing returned to normal, she crumpled the bag in disgust and threw it onto Main Street.

"Better pick that up, Miss Neil," Barrett warned. "I'd hate to have to handcuff you again, this time for littering. Oh, and there's a two-hundred dollar fine." He tapped the handcuffs in his pocket with a smirk.

"You think this is *funny*?" Lainey fumed, storming off the boardwalk to grab the crumpled bag. She threw it so hard into a trash can beside the bar that it made a thump. "As far as I can tell, my career is pretty much in the gutter right now. All because I tried to be brave!"

Barrett crossed his arms and gazed at her patiently. "No one ever said there aren't consequences for standing up for yourself," he pointed out. "Deciding on your own destiny doesn't exactly make you popular with users. You told me Ron wanted you to play the same damn character from *Horse Feathers* a decade later—keeping you in some creepy time capsule for a fat paycheck. If that's what it takes to please this guy, going your own way might be a blessing in disguise."

Lainey gritted her teeth, slicing her molars back and forth. "The thing that stings the most is that he obviously thinks my career has tanked," she moaned softly. "He has no faith in me. Apparently, I'm *baggage*—"

"No," Barrett challenged her. "You're carrying your *own weight* right now. There's a difference. The truth is, you're not toting *his* baggage anymore. Don't let him convince you otherwise if he does shit for your career," Barrett said. "He's been syphoning off twenty percent of your earnings for years, right? And now he just proved he's not the least bit loyal to you?"

Lainey sighed. "*Loyal* qualifies as a foreign word in Hollywood," she replied. "Aside from Deb Griffin, I hardly know if I'd recognize it if I saw it."

Barrett became quiet. Despite his guarded expression, the raw way he glanced at Lainey held a longing that took her breath away.

"Wouldn't you know *loyalty* if it stared you in the face?" he said sharply. The hint of bitterness in his tone pierced Lainey's heart. He shifted his gaze to the boardwalk for a second before reaching to open the bar door.

"C'mon," he urged, "Harper needs your support right now. Maybe you can show her and the rest of the crew what it means to be *loyal*."

The bite in his words disturbed Lainey, and she desperately wished she could swallow back what she'd said. "Barrett," she added, "I-I'm sorry all I did right now was talk about myself, while you've been standing here generously listening all along—"

To Lainey's astonishment, he cupped the back of her neck and pulled her in for a bold kiss before she could utter another word. In some strange way, she felt as if he were erasing the Hollywood bubble of self-absorption that surrounded her—

and perhaps even caged her—while his ardent kiss was forcing her to live in the moment.

This moment...

Barrett pressed his chest against hers so firmly she could feel the throb of his heart beating through his shirt, making goosebumps dance up and down her skin.

"For God's sake, Lainey," he said as he broke away, his warm breath hovering over her cheek. He peered into her eyes with a searing gaze. "Can't you enjoy yourself without thinking about Hollywood for a second? From what I've seen of the musical chairs of crazies that pop in and out of your life, there's always a good reason to hit the roof over another asshole. But in my world, I deal with death and crime and tragedy every day. If I weren't doing security for *Skystone Canyon* right now, I'd be out there busting a meth ring that's responsible for killing at least three people." He brazenly laid his hand upon her chest, feeling her heart leap against his palm, while her pulse quickened. "And last time I checked," he smiled, "you're spectacularly beautiful, you're heart's still beating, and you're standing right in front of me." His eyes poured into hers with an admiration that made sparks tingle to her toes. "As far as I'm concerned, that makes for a pretty damn great day."

Lainey's breath hitched in her throat.

Barrett was right—

When it came to tragedies in this world, standing on her own two feet for her career without Ron to tangle with hardly measured up to what Barrett considered "tough". All at once, she felt embarrassed she'd fallen into the rabbit hole of self-pity right in front of him. Throwing back her shoulders to retain some semblance of dignity, she opened her mouth to reply, when Barrett gently placed his finger over her lips.

"Save it for the tequila," he said, a smile teasing his lips. "For one night, maybe we can just…*be*. Think you can handle that?"

"Well, knowing me, that'll probably be a struggle," Lainey giggled. "But I'm willing to give it a shot."

"Good," Barrett replied. "Now let's get inside."

When Barrett opened the bar door, to Lainey's surprise, the entire place fell quiet. She knew she wasn't a big enough star to elicit such a response, especially since she hadn't been on a popular show since she was a teen. Curious, she watched as the men and women who'd been milling around with drinks in their hands stood aside and made way for Barrett to walk past them like the parting of the Red Sea. Lainey scanned the bar, wondering if their odd behavior was because of their intimidation from his status as a police officer. Then she happened to spot a large-screen TV on the opposite wall. There was Barrett on *American Rodeo Highlights* on the RFD channel in a rodeo arena, roping a calf within only three strides of his horse's gallop after breaking from the gate. He leaped down from Sand and tied off the calf's hooves whiplash fast. Then he threw up his arms to indicate his finish while the crowd thundered in applause.

"That's how it's done folks!" the rodeo announcer burst. "Barrett Iron Feather wins his fourth national belt buckle in the tiedown competition. We'd hardly expect anything less of this Colorado roping sensation!"

Barrett sent a threatening sideways glance to the bartender, who instantly pulled out a remote and turned down the TV.

Despite the muted volume, however, all of the other cowboys in the bar tipped their hats and nodded as he walked by.

Barrett turned to Lainey. "Guess loyalty and respect ain't so hard to come by in this part of the world," he remarked. "Maybe you Hollywood types should go to more rodeos." He nodded at the bottles of liquor lined up against the bar. "What's your pleasure, Miss Neil?"

"After the day I've had, I'm thinking a hefty Margarita about the size of your boot, cowboy," she teased. "By the way," her voice took on a more serious tone, "you never told me you're a *star*, Barrett Iron Feather. I saw the way people reacted to you walking in here. I think *awe* might be the appropriate term."

Barrett swung his arm around her gave her a squeeze. "Believe me, I am damn proud that the hard-working ranching people of Bandits Hollow call me their friend. If I've managed to earn their esteem, I am truly grateful. But Lainey, you hung in there today and certainly earned my respect. And speaking of respect," he nodded toward a teenage girl who'd just stepped inside the bar, "isn't that Heather, one of the extras Easton Wolfe hit on? We don't won't a repeat happening with anyone else in this bar."

"Oh heavens," Lainey gasped, "she can't be in here! I'd better escort her to our hotel down the street. I promised to keep her safe—"

Barrett clutched her elbow before Lainey could march away. "Legally, she *can* be here under the supervision of an adult." He turned Lainey to view Heather's mother across the room, standing near enough to watch her, but not close enough to embarrass her daughter.

"Well, I gave my word I'd keep an eye out for her, anyway. See?" Lainey poked Barrett in the ribs, "some of us Hollywood types *can* be loyal after all."

"Good to hear," Barrett replied, his eyes sweeping the room out of police habit for anyone who might bother Heather. Lainey spotted the patrol-officer concern in his gaze, and she elbowed him.

"Look who's obsessed with work now!" she smirked. "And I think I know the perfect cure. Aren't they dancing in that room over there?" She pointed to an overflow room in the back where there was an old jukebox pumping out music. "I'm going to grab Heather right now and show her some fun. That way she won't be out of my sight."

Barrett had just mentioned something to the bartender when Lainey seized him by the hand. She wove around customers in the bar until she reached Heather.

"Hey Heather, wanna join us for country line dancing?"

Heather glanced up shyly, a blush coloring her cheeks that the star of *Skystone Canyon* was giving her attention. "I, um, I don't really know how," she admitted.

"Neither do I!" replied Lainey with a grin. "Let's give it a try—it might be fun!"

She clasped the girl's hand and pulled her over with Barrett to the overflow room, filing in line with the other dancers. Lainey and Heather awkwardly stumbled their way through a few moves, until Barrett positioned himself between them.

"Follow my lead, ladies," he said in low tone, thrusting his leg out for a kick in time with the music, then stepping behind before going forward with another kick. Lainey and Heather copied his motions, moving to the side and turning in rhythm to the beat.

"Hey, this is fun!" Heather giggled, trying to add the right hip motion even though she missed a few steps.

It didn't go unnoticed by Barrett that Lainey giggled too, especially when his body swung into a rotation followed by a boot slide.

"Well, Officer Iron Feather," Lainey winked, "you're pretty damn good at this! Who knew you had smooth moves lurking inside you?"

Barrett looped his thumbs in his jeans and turned to her without missing a beat. "When you grow up in Bandits Hollow, you gotta find something to pass the evenings. Throw your boot up higher like this, Lainey," he instructed, giving her a wicked outlaw smile that she found heart-stoppingly sexy. "You look nice when you kick up your heels for a change."

Just as he swiveled into another set of kicks, the music began to die down. Harper Stone walked in front of the jukebox toting a microphone in her hand. Yet she wasn't wearing her usual black, femme fatale outfit. This time, she had on torn blue jeans and cowboy boots with a red rodeo shirt dotted by rhinestones. She turned around and slipped a couple of quarters in the jukebox and carefully pressed the buttons. As Tammy Wynette's vintage tune *Stand By Your Man* began to fill the room, Harper lifted the microphone to her lips.

"I'd like to thank each and every one of you for coming out here tonight," she announced, her words echoing into the main room of the bar as well, "in support of the *Skystone Canyon* film project. And I want you to know that every actor and member of the crew is going to get an additional bonus in their paychecks this week that comes straight from *me* as a gesture of gratitude for your loyalty for this film."

Cheers filled the bar. Yet Lainey couldn't help noticing that Harper's diamond-crusted Rolex watch was *missing*—

From across the room, Lainey met Harper's gaze. She held up her arm and tapped her wrist where the watch should be. Harper simply gave her a wink.

That's when Lainey knew for certain Harper had pawned the watch to reward the film crew.

Touched beyond belief, Lainey lifted her fingers to make a heart symbol and blew Harper a kiss. As far as she was concerned, it would be their little secret.

To Lainey surprise, Harper motioned for her to join her in front of the jukebox. Nervous, Lainey walked up to her, when Harper wrapped an arm around her shoulders. The bartender headed toward them holding a large, ceramic cowboy boot, the kind normally used for a kitschy, retro planter. He handed it to Harper.

"Tonight, I am handing out this very special boot," Harper said with a big grin, "containing a half gallon of Margarita with the highest grade tequila for our dependable and oh-so-passionate star, Miss Lainey Neil!"

Stunned, Lainey shot a glance at Barrett, who gave her a proud smirk.

"Sometimes it's hard to be a woman, giving your love to just one film," Harper broke out in song along with the music as she handed the boot to Lainey. "You'll have bad times, and you'll have good times, doin' everything you can. But if you love the movie, you'll keep going, honey, even though it's hard to make a stand. And because you love it, you'll be oh so proud of it, 'cause after all it's still your film."

Harper stretched out her arms dramatically, belting out her version of the chorus:

> *Stand by your film,*
> *And show the world you love it,*
> *Keep giving all the love you can,*
> *Stand by your film!*

By the time Harper reached the final words, everyone in the bar had linked arms and was singing along with her, swaying to the tune. When the music stopped, more hoots and hollers were followed by applause. Lainey held the boot up high above her head with a smile as Harper took a bow.

"Now y'all have fun tonight," Harper called out her petitioned in a twangy tone, "because I'm gonna work you like hell tomorrow!"

The actors and crew whooped with more applause and then returned to their drinks and dancing as Lainey headed toward Heather to escort her back to mother. Still toting her cowboy boot, Lainey met up with Barrett and sat down at the bar.

"Looks like I have some work ahead of me!" she laughed as she set the clunky ceramic boot on the bar counter. "Would you consider helping me a little?"

"Only if you let me take you home again. Deal?" Barrett replied. "After that boot, you might have trouble finding your way."

"Sure," Lainey said, tipping the boot to take an awkward

sip. "But where do you go at night, Officer Iron Feather?" she asked, curious. "Back to that magnificent house on the Iron Feather brothers' ranch? Nice digs, if you ask me."

"Not tonight," Barrett sighed, scanning the room in surveillance mode again. When his gaze fell on Heather safely near her mother, he appeared to relax a bit. "After I reported the suspicious stampede today to the police chief, he assigned me to stay at the Golden Wagon Hotel."

"You reported the stampede?" Lainey said, floored. "Why?"

"Because Cayden Hart could easily have been killed," Barrett informed her. "If that occurred near the set, where a known police officer and cattleman was patrolling, imagine what else could happen. The police chief wants me to stay at the hotel tonight, just in case."

Lainey rolled her eyes. "All that stuff—the bur under the saddle, the broken harness, the stray poppers—they're haphazard incidents. Do you really still believe we're somehow in danger?"

"Damn straight," Barrett replied in a somber tone. "I hate to dampen your fun night, Lainey, but at the station we follow the rule of threes. Three is a definite pattern, not an accident anymore, so the police chief isn't taking chances. Hopefully, we're wrong, like you said," he glanced at Lainey with a sexy half smile, "and the worst thing that happens at the hotel is that we might spy one of Bandits Hollow's ghosts."

"Ghosts?" she replied, threading her fingers together.

"Don't worry," Barrett added nonchalantly, "last time I heard, they don't hurt anyone. They just make quite a racket."

19

G hosts…

   Lainey scooted beneath the covers in her bed at the Golden Wagon Hotel as Barrett's casual mention of the word kept circling in her brain. Okay, she admitted to herself, so I'm a bit tipsy from the tequila tonight, and maybe I'm a little paranoid. She'd never felt fully comfortable sleeping in this old relic of a hotel from the first day she'd arrived, which looked to her like a living museum to Bandits Hollow's gold rush past—and to its supposed spooks. She pulled the covers up to her nose for comfort, peering warily into the dark recesses of her room.

   It didn't help matters that the old Victorian hotel had ornate molding and vintage wallpaper, befitting the kind of late-night movie locations where spirits always seem to lurk. Lainey's mind wandered over the outlaw history she'd heard about in Bandits Hollow, speculating that surely someone had gotten shot in this hotel at least once or twice. On top of that, a taxidermied bear adorned one of the walls with its teeth bared and paws extended, as if ready to strike. Apparently it hadn't been shot by a hunter, but rather had lost a fight with a mountain lion half a century ago in the town square, according to the engraved words on the brass plaque. Nevertheless, its dark glass eyes gleamed with an ominous stare.

"You're being silly," Lainey whispered, berating herself. "That poor, stuffed animal can't hurt anyone. Besides, what would a bear ghost do even if it did prowl around the hotel? Steal honey?"

But still…

Just to be on the safe side, Lainey decided to fill her room with exuberant sounds by singing a few bars of *Stand By Your Man* to keep nagging notions of the supernatural out of her mind. Occasionally, she inserted the words to *Stand By Your Bear*, on the off chance that it might make a bear spirit roaming through the hotel happy. Though she hadn't finished her bootful of Margarita that night, at that moment she dearly wished she'd downed the whole thing and passed out—then falling asleep wouldn't be a struggle. After all, it wouldn't be the worst fate in the world to be carried home drunk by Barrett Iron Feather, would it?

A blush flared on Lainey's cheeks at the thought, though there was no one else in the room. She sighed, unable to deny the fact that after all these years, she was still wildly attracted to Barrett—just like when she was fourteen. And Lord knows, he'd *kissed* her! With the kinds of kisses that make your toes curl and send your emotions swirling into warm, delicious fantasies…

Just like the fantasy she used to have that they'd keep in touch, after he promised a decade ago that he'd be loyal and write to her—

Loyal.

There was that word again…

Why, oh why, hadn't she ever received a single letter that he claimed he'd sent? Was he really telling the truth, or feeding her a line? Lainey had seen for herself the deep longing in Barrett's eyes when he looked at her. Not to mention the admiration he seemed to have for her acts of courage and for her full-bloom, womanly figure now.

Yet she had to admit, half a dozen actors had looked at her that same way—it was written in their scripts. They had simply been following directions…

Lainey shook her head. She was old enough to know by now that on-set relationships never went anywhere positive. Which unfortunately might include Barrett, too. Perhaps his passion for being a police officer lent itself to the same kind of adrenaline rush actors experience, only for the people he was supposed to protect. Such passion was merely part of his job description…

Including those heavenly kisses?

But who wouldn't want to steal a few lip locks from the star of a Hollywood film? Think of Barrett's bragging rights to his rodeo pals! Like usual, Lainey realized, mixing work with pleasure is a slippery slope that might never lead anywhere.

Good grief, Lainey yawned, I'm wearing myself out with these kinds of thoughts. Face it, if Barrett had really wanted to get a hold of me over the years, he would have! And *now* he starts flirting like Johnny on the spot? Lainey winced at her gullibility and stretched out her arms, glad she was finally succumbing to fatigue. She reached over to the nightstand to turn off the lamp and snuggled deeper beneath the covers, sinking into her pillow for some much-needed shut eye.

Several hours passed, and Lainey's dreams became filled with a jumbled montage of the day's events. A herd of cattle dashing across a pasture. Local bar patrons kicking up their cowboy boots and line dancing. A famous Hollywood icon dressed like the sweetheart of the rodeo, belting out a country tune in front of a jukebox.

Eventually, her dreams slipped into lovely images of the snow-dotted peaks and dark green forests that surrounded Bandits Hollow. She had no idea how long she'd been asleep when the call of an owl ripped through her dreams. All at once, Lainey saw the silhouette of a man in the moonlight. The full moon was so bright it etched the outline of his body in platinum hues. The tall stranger with broad shoulders and Native American features looked just like...

Dillon. Barrett's older brother.

Except he was wearing a black hat with a flat brim and a dark coat with brass buttons that glinted in the moonlight. On his cheek was a heavy scar...

To Lainey's confusion, the stranger in her dream held out a piece of turquoise in his hand that glinted in the moonlight. The stone was a pure, perfect blue, without a hint of matrix.

"*Ha'dish'ai,*" he said, nodding at her. "I sing for you."

The man lifted his voice in a rhythmic chant, his tones rising and falling to the beat of a faraway drum. For a long time, his song continued, filling Lainey's heart with an odd peace she didn't quite understand. When he finished his song, the man smiled, revealing large, uneven teeth.

"It's your song," he told her. "The sky stone song."

The moment he spoke those words, the darkness around him began to lift as the moon slipped from view, as though his voice had the power to clear shadows and bring forth the dawn. Soon, the sun inched over the horizon, tinting Lainey's dream in golden hues.

"*Hayiitka*," the man told her mysteriously. The glow on the horizon slowly warmed his rugged features.

Yet his utterance startled Lainey—

She recognized that word: *Hayiitka*. Barrett had told her it meant sunrise in Apache, the name of his brother's chestnut horse.

Then the man fell silent for a long time, as though allowing the effect of his song to trickle into her soul. Finally, his eyes narrowed, and Lainey had the distinct, uncomfortable feeling that he could peer into her heart.

"He loves you," the man said, to her astonishment. "He is not cold, like his older brother. He rages hot. He burns like *jígonaa'áí*, the sun. Such burning in his heart can never die."

The man lifted his gaze to the brightening blue horizon.

"To him, you are the sky."

At that moment, a great horned owl alighted on the man's shoulder. It chortled softly, and the man dipped his head as though carefully listening.

"Our people have a story," he stated, his dark, obsidian eyes staring intently into hers. "Those who near the sun run into many tests from evil ones. Only those who endure are given bows of rainbows and arrows of lightning. Mark my word, the son of *jigonaa'ái*—the sun—will protect you from evil ones. But only if you listen to him. And to the stone's song…"

The man's voice trailed off, and he gazed at the turquoise stone in his hand. Without warning, he tossed the stone toward Lainey. She watched as it arced in air and began to expand to fill her field of vision, painting the whole world a beautiful, perfect blue. Before she knew it, she was tumbling end over end in that blue—falling or rising—she couldn't tell. All she knew was that she felt as if she'd *become* the blue—protected by this stone, this sky, this great expanse of infinite blue light. She heard the man's voice again.

"Remember *shich'choonii*, listen to him—to his love. And to the sky stones."

The insistent call of an owl echoed through her thoughts, and Lainey's lashes began to flutter. She opened her eyes, only to be met by darkness all around. When the owl sounded again, she bolted up in bed, spying a great horned owl at her window, which had been left open to enjoy the crisp mountain air. The owl issued another long, lonely call as it lifted its broad wings and soared over her bed.

Lainey let out a blood-curdling scream.

Petrified, she sank beneath her covers. Within seconds, a sharp pounding erupted at her door. Lainey heard her named called, but she was too frozen to reply. All at once, a crash thundered as if someone had kicked the door in. Her bed covers were yanked from her face.

There was Barrett, hovering over her in the dark, his gaze filled with a world of concern.

"You okay, Lainey?" he burst, staring into her eyes. He

scanned the room for signs of danger before sitting down on her bed.

"Th-there was a man, and then th-there was an owl," she stammered, her eyes wide in shock. "I know it must sound crazy, but somehow I feel like it wasn't a dream. Like he was really here," she insisted, searching Barrett's face. "The man—he told a story about reaching toward the sun and being protected from evil ones by his song and turquoise. One of his words sounded like your brother's name for his horse. And another word sounded like, you know, the kinds of things your mother used to say."

"My mother?" replied Barrett, thoroughly confused. He leaned in closer. "What do you mean?"

"When the man finished talking, he called me *shich'choonii*. I don't know why, but it reminded me of your mother when she visited you at camp. When she used to hug you and say things in Apache."

"Jicarilla," Barrett nodded, his eyes narrowing. "That word —it's an Apache term of endearment."

He glanced down at the bedspread for a moment. To Lainey's surprise, he picked up a long, banded gray feather and held it to her.

"It-it's from an owl, isn't it?" she said, her voice trembling a little.

"Lainey," Barrett replied gently, "tell me, what did this man look like?"

"Your brother," Lainey answered, clutching her arms around her waist to try and keep from shaking. "He looked like Dillon. Only he had a big scar on his cheek."

Barrett's eyes grew wide. "Iron Feather," he said, barely above a whisper.

His words sent goosebumps down Lainey's spine. "B-But why would he visit *me*?" she asked, remembering that odd silhouette she'd seen against a boulder on the day they were horseback riding and they'd taken the Thieves Trail. The memory of the dark, ink-like stain on the rock still rattled her. "Why on earth would his spirit bother to sing me a song and—"

"Because he's *protecting* you," Barrett asserted in a low, adamant tone.

Barrett fell quiet, his dark eyes boring into hers. For the life of her, Lainey wished she could hear his thoughts, how he could possibly make sense of these peculiar events. Yet though their eyes met, and he appeared consumed with concern, a remote part him seemed a million miles away. It was as if his soul were a distant star that burned brightly, but one who's light he rarely shared closely with other people. Not because he didn't feel—but perhaps because he felt too much. Even so, it was a star Lainey longed to reach.

Barrett startled her by leaning beside her pillow and picking up a small stone. He held it to the moonlight that streamed through the window so Lainey could see.

It was a piece of turquoise.

Gently, he smoothed Lainey's hair and grased her temples, staring into her eyes. For a moment, he rubbed his thumbs against her cheeks before glancing at the window as though at any moment something—or someone—might appear. Then without a word, he walked over to shut the door. Returning to the bed, he opened up Lainey's bedspread and crawled beneath the covers beside her. He slipped his hand in hers.

"Lainey," he said in the darkness.

"Yes?" she replied, relishing the strong, comforting grip of his hand.

"I'm not leaving your side."

Barrett glanced at the window again and held up the piece of turquoise before tucking it into his pocket.

"Whether you understand it or not," he added, "I have all the evidence I need to focus on keeping you safe. In the morning, I'll repair the door for Nell Granger before heading to the set, and then I'll have Nell bill me. But from now on, Miss Neil, you're staying with me."

Lainey squeezed his hand, then pulled it up to her lips for a kiss.

"Okay," she said.

Barrett rolled over in the bed and wrapped his arms around her. He held her close with all his might.

"Goodnight, Miss Neil," he said softly.

"Goodnight, Officer Iron Feather."

❧ 20 ❧

Lainey squinted at the early morning sunshine that streamed through Harper Stone's trailer window before she leaned over and threw up into the trash can. Harper handed her a warm wash cloth to wipe off her mouth.

"How could I get food poisoning last night, when no one else did?" Lainey moaned, seizing the washcloth to rid the last remnants of vomit from her face. "It's not fair! God, the taste that lingers in my mouth is awful."

Harper nodded, her eyes covered by dark sunglasses even inside the trailer. She reached down to a plastic storage bin beside the kitchen table and opened it, pulling out a bottle of Bourbon.

"Here, honey," she asserted, handing the bottle to Lainey. "Swish a little of this in your mouth and gargle, then spit it out in the sink."

Lainey's eyes popped. "Harper!" She stared at the label, "I got rid of all those bottles! I thought you were going to give this up—"

"Darling," Harper whipped off her sunglasses to reveal bloodshot eyes, "you didn't really think I'd abandon the longest-running relationship of my *life*, now did you?" She winked at Lainey. "Don't worry, I got the hint that I could cut back a little. It's just that some attachments are meant to endure." She shot a glance out the window at Barrett, who sauntered over to Sand and swung into the saddle, sitting tall on his horse in the early morning light. Harper smiled a little. "Like you and that goddamned handsome cowboy. Not that I'm jealous or anything," she added.

Lainey's cheeks flushed with embarrassment, and she coughed, wiping her lips once again. "D-Do you really think we're meant for each other?" she asked.

Harper rolled her eyes. "God, I hope so. Because we have a kissing scene today. And food poisoning or not, the camera needs to capture your face while that cowboy cop stands in for Cayden. In other words, pioneer girl, you gotta make it look hot." She turned to Lainey with a smirk. "But if you have any trouble at all, I'd be happy to give your cowboy cop kissing lessons."

Lainey threw back another gargle of Bourbon before spitting into the sink. "I think I can handle it now," she promised, patting her stomach that was exhausted from lurching. She slid a glance at Harper. "But keep the Bourbon handy, just in case."

After rinsing her washcloth and going over her face one

last time, Lainey followed Harper out of the trailer to head over to the camera area.

"Oh my gosh!" cried Deb when she saw Lainey, toting her cosmetic case. "I heard you'd gotten a stomach bug this morning. You all right?" She opened her case and whipped out some cotton balls to repair Lainey's makeup.

"Food poisoning," grumbled Lainey. "I think I barfed it all out already. Thank God Harper had an extra trash can."

"You poor thing," Deb shook her head. "Guess it could happen to anybody."

"Yeah, but it didn't," Lainey replied. "Isn't that odd? No one else who went to the bar last night had any problems."

Deb stopped dabbing Lainey's face. She briefly surveyed the other crew members. "Do you think it might have happened on the set, then?" she whispered. "Could someone have tainted your lunch?" She nodded at one of the sound operators who'd remained on the crew. "Derrick over there has worked for six of Easton's films. I heard him talking to Cayden the other day about all the parties they've been together. Nasty payback?"

Lainey shifted her gaze to Derrick. The young man with blonde hair was known for his cocky attitude and even cockier behavior, constantly pranking his guy friends at work and accompanying them after hours to chase women. Though he was a member of the crew, and he was supposed to wear period clothing on the set, he always showed up in tie-died t-shirts and torn jeans anyway, with the obligatory ball cap turned backwards on his head. But as far as Lainey knew, he was a good soundman who took his job seriously. Could this guy be capable of sabotage?

Or was she simply letting her dream last night get the best of her? Did Iron Feather really need to protect her?

Lainey shook her head, uncertain whether there was anything to worry about.

"Another person I've never trusted is Jonathan," Deb confided. "He claimed once that he was Easton's better-looking wing man who pulled in all the chicks. Like he's God's gift to the universe. You wouldn't believe the stuff I hear on the set while I'm waiting to do makeup."

"Jonathan?" Lainey echoed. "He's a toad! He wouldn't even be good looking if he finally lost forty pounds. What is it with these creepy guys who are so loyal to Easton, like it's a badge for bad behavior?"

"Birds of a feather," Deb remarked, giving each one of them the side eye.

"*Skystone Canyon* actors, time for your marks!" yelled an assistant.

Deb patted Lainey's face. "You're all set, my dear." She dug into her cosmetic case and handed Lainey two pink tabs of Pepto-Bismal. "But you might want to chew on these, just in case."

"Thanks," Lainey said. She took a deep breath, watching Harper in the distance convince Barrett to get off his horse in order to be a stand-in for the scene. "I shouldn't complain about kissing a handsome police officer. At least I don't have to deal with Cayden at this hour."

"There is a God," Deb laughed. "Now go get 'em, tiger."

Lainey walked across the grass and reached the spot where a red X was spray painted on the ground, waiting for Barrett. As he approached, he gave her a darkened stare.

Clearly, he wasn't exactly happy about being asked to do the scene.

Has he heard rumors about me vomiting this morning? Lainey wondered.

"I promise I gargled with Bourbon—twice," Lainey assured him when he reached her side. "I think I got this bug out of my system. So you won't be in any danger of, you know, a crappy tasting experience."

Barrett dipped his hat to her with a slight smile teasing his lips. "Make no mistake about it, Miss Neil," he said in a husky voice that she found irresistibly sexy, "I would kiss you even if you were dipped in motor oil."

The crew laughed, and several of the men gave him a fist pump.

"But if you *ever* let my brothers Dillon and Lander know that I'm standing in for the soft love interest in this movie," Barrett warned, "I will personally have you tarred and feathered." He gave her a wink. "Before I swipe the next kiss, of course."

The crew applauded Barrett's good sportsmanship while an assistant turned his shoulders at just the right angle so the camera could shoot the back of his head and catch Lainey's expression full on.

"I don't think there's too much to worry about," Lainey assured him, "since we can't show your face. But just in case," Lainey turned his chin a bit more to make the task less potentially embarrassing. "There, perfect."

"No, *you're* perfect," Barrett smiled, gazing into her eyes. With the morning sun's glow on Lainey's features, she looked to him like a dewy angel. "I hope they're not in a hurry to get

rolling," he whispered, "because I could look at your face all
day long."

Lainey blushed just as Harper gave the command to start
the shoot.

"Okay, cowboy cop," Harper hollered, checking the film's
storyboard easel, "you've just rescued this woman from
renegade cattle rustlers, who nearly took your lives. And you're
overcome with passion, so you seize her by the shoulders and
give her a kiss. Action!"

"Nope," Barrett boldly turned around and faced Harper
while the cameras were rolling, defying her direction. "That
ain't how it's done, ma'am. First of all, if you look back at the
dailies, Ada Holdwel picked up one of the rifles from a man
I'd taken down and started shooting at the rustlers her own
damn self." Barrett turned and smiled at Lainey. "She didn't
need my rescuing—I just butted in to try and impress her. And
second of all," he said loud enough for Harper and the crew
to hear, "what you just told me ain't how any self-respecting
cowboy kisses the love of his life."

"It isn't?" said Harper, visibly startled. She circled her
finger in the air for the crew to keep filming. "Then show us
how it's done, cowboy!"

"Gladly, ma'am," replied Barrett. Without a word, he took
several strides back from Lainey to start the scene. When
Harper cried "Action" again, Barrett began to march toward
Lainey like a man on a mission. Then he threw his hat to the
ground and scooped Lainey up in his arms, holding her close
to his chest like his greatest treasure. He proceeded to kiss her
with every ounce of his being, as if it were the last time on
earth he might ever see her—yet at the same time, with the

possibility of beginning of a whole new life. In Barrett's kiss was the promise of his soul as he poured himself into Lainey's lips, making an electric current charge like lightning bolts down her spine. When Harper yelled "Cut!" Barrett gently broke free and set Lainey to her feet, still reeling.

The crew exploded in adulation, making Lainey giggle. She did a small curtsy.

"That, Miss Harper," Barrett said, while an assistant fetched his hat and handed it to him, "is a how a *real* cowboy kisses a woman that he fully intends to keep."

"Well, praise the Lord and pass the ammunition!" hooted Harper. "Damned if that wasn't the best cowboy kiss ever caught on film! Now I know what I been missing. Got any brothers, cowboy?" she purred as she walked up to Lainey and Barrett and gave each of them a high five.

"He does," Lainey smiled, "but I hear they're a little on the wild side."

"Perfect!" replied Harper. "Next time they're in town, give me a shout." She turned to the rest of the crew. "We'll take a break now and prepare for the next scene after lunch. Great job, folks!"

"Yes, that was fantastic," Lainey heard a voice remark from behind her as Harper headed to the storyboard easel to review the following scenes. Lainey whipped around, her mouth dropping in shock.

"Chris?" she gasped, staring at the face of her ex-boyfriend. "What the hell are you doing here?"

The man who wasn't much taller than Lainey with red hair and surprisingly cute dimples for being in his twenties smiled and gave a little shrug. "Aw, I was just in Aspen vacationing and I heard you were down here, so I thought I'd drop by. But I guess the real question is, what are *you* doing here?"

Dumbfounded, Lainey searched his face. "What do you mean?"

Chris wrapped an arm around her shoulder and glared at Barrett. "Would you mind excusing us for a second? We have the same agent—"

"*Had* the same agent," Barrett snapped, clenching his fists. "Lainey, if this man is bothering you in any way, as head of security, it's my job—"

"No, it's okay," Lainey replied, holding out her hands to calm Barrett and avoid trouble. She couldn't help noticing the way his fingers hovered over the handcuffs he kept in his pocket. "We used to be on shows together," she explained to Barrett, sending Chris a warning look. "I'll just catch up with him for a minute and then go get lunch, okay?"

Barrett tipped his hat and turned to head back to his horse Sand, glancing over his shoulder to check on Lainey's progress. It made her feel good that he was keeping her in his sights. She walked off with Chris toward some folding chairs and offered him one to sit down beside her.

"Lainey," Chris said right out of the gate, "I've heard rumors about this movie from hell you're stuck in. How Easton Wolfe got arrested and Cayden Hart took off. By the way, what's with the no makeup thing? Everyone I know is worried about you—"

"I have light film makeup on," Lainey defended herself. "It's simply more natural for a pioneer role than what you're used to. And what do you mean by *everyone*? Did Ron put you up to coming here? How dare he, after bailing on me."

Chris shook his head. "No, it's just that, you know how it is —word travels fast in the entertainment industry. Like the fact that you've been blowing off opportunities from Ron for a film that's frankly bound to fail."

Lainey narrowed her gaze. "What do you know about this film? It's a great story, and—"

"A flop waiting to happen. Listen, Lainey, great stories don't bring in the bucks. Great entertainment brings in the bucks. And that's the real reason I'm here." He smiled and tenderly brushed Lainey's wayward hair from her eyes. "I have an opportunity for you. There's a position open now on *Life On The Rocks*. I'm sure you're aware that it's a massive, reality show hit. This would mean a huge break for you—but you'd have to be willing to start Monday."

Lainey's jaw nearly hit the ground. "Chris," she said, flabbergasted, "the slot is open on your reality show because the last guy died of an overdose. That was only three days ago —it was all over the news! How could you be so cold as to try and fill it already? Has there even been a funeral yet? I have a word for you: it's called hiatus. I'm sure your fans would let a couple of months go by so you and the cast can grieve."

"Well, to be honest, we were never very tight," Chris replied.

"I don't believe this!" Lainey burst. "The whole reason you're here is to try and muscle me to go on your sleazy reality show about child stars who've hit the skids? Where if a person overdoses it's just Russian roulette, because there's plenty more where they came from? Do you hear yourself?"

"Lainey, I've banked a million bucks this year," Chris stated flatly. "And given the financial trouble you had with your dad, I thought—"

"You thought wrong!" Lainey fumed, barely able to believe her ears. She stood up, ready to leave, when Chris grasped her by the arm. He set his hands on her shoulders and looked into her eyes. For a second, he glanced behind his shoulder before returning his gaze to Lainey.

"Don't you remember the good old days," he said sweetly, "when you and I were on the cover of *Tiger Beat Magazine* practically every month? As a couple, we were the talk of the country. You can have that again, Lainey. It's within your reach."

Chris nervously checked behind him again, which Lainey thought might be due to his concern over Barrett—a rational fear. She sighed and returned his gaze.

"I don't want to be sixteen again, Chris. No amount of money is worth that to me. In case you forgot, my life was horrible back then—constantly controlled by my father and emotionally abused by so-called professionals. I don't care what you or others think of *Skystone Canyon*—it's helped me get my life back on track, doing roles I believe in."

"C'mon, Lainey," Chris urged, giving her a soft peck on the forehead. "People want to see us back together again. And I promise if you come on Monday, there'll be hefty bonus waiting for you. In fact," he dug into his pocket for his cell phone, tapping on a social media app until the right picture came into view, "I already posted your photo to prove I saw you today. Look at the number of likes on Instagram! People are going crazy!"

Lainey blinked several times in shock. Chris had snapped a picture of her in her calico prairie dress right before her kissing scene, and the photo had already earned over a hundred thousand likes.

"See?" gushed Chris. "Everyone wants Chris and Lainey to be an item again."

Before she knew it, Chris had yanked her closer and leaned his head next to hers, snapping a photo of himself grinning beside Lainey in the same frame. He hit the post button and his phone began to blow up with likes and comments. Chris laughed, pleased with himself, and nodded at the cameraman in front of him—

The cameraman?

It was then Lainey realized that the guy wandering around with a hand-held video camera on his shoulder wasn't doing prep shots for *Skystone Canyon*. He was with Chris, and this so-called "reunion" was all being filmed as a promo to boost his show *Life On The Rocks*.

Lainey held out her hand to block her face from view, and that's all it took—

Within seconds, Barrett had galloped Sand straight for her and slid his horse to a stop, bounding out of the saddle to grab Chris by the collar. He shoved Chris into his buddy's lens.

"Did you get a good shot of his face now, asshole?" Barrett growled at the cameraman while Chris squirmed.

"I can sue you for this!" Chris squealed, flailing his arms, until Barrett pinned his hands behind him and cuffed them.

"Not if they don't find the body," Barrett replied, making Chris' face turn to ash. He pointed his finger at the cameraman. "If you don't get your ass off the *Skystone Canyon* set this second, you're next," Barrett promised.

The cameraman dashed off to the parking area on the other side of the set, quickly tossing his equipment inside a BMW. He managed to hop behind the steering wheel while Barrett hauled Chris over to the car and yanked opened the passenger door. Unlocking the handcuffs, he threw Chris inside. Then he tipped his hat to the two men with a stern gaze.

"That's an official Bandits Hollow goodbye, gentlemen. Don't ever let this town see your faces again."

The BMW peeled off, kicking up so much dust from careening down Main Street that for a moment Barrett was obscured from view. Feeling fragile from the whole ordeal, not to mention the trial with her stomach earlier, Lainey walked over to Deb Griffin and laid her head on her shoulder. Deb gently patted her on the cheek.

"You know, sometimes the entertainment business isn't pretty," Lainey sighed. "But I have to admire the way Barrett got rid of those guys. Do you think Ron pressured Chris to harass me so I might come back to him?"

Deb thought about it for a moment, leveling her gaze at Derrick and Jonathan, who were bantering with each other and sharing laughs. "Who knows," she shrugged, giving another crew member the once over. "Didn't Joey over there work in lighting on the *Horse Feathers* set for a while? Maybe he tipped Chris off for a finder's fee or something."

Lainey squinted at Joey, who was carrying a huge light fixture onto a flat bed trailer to get ready for transport for the next scene. Releasing a weary breath, she folded her arms in resignation.

"All I know," Lainey confessed, "is that people you can trust in this industry are few and far between. And to be honest, I can count them all on one hand."

"Barrett, after everything that…happened…in my hotel room last night," Lainey mentioned awkwardly, twisting her fingers, "is it possible to take a break from staying at the Golden Wagon Hotel?" She watched the other crew members idly walking down Main Street on their way to the hotel after filming was finished for the day, talking and laughing with one another. A clench of envy gripped her at their carefree attitudes. "Aren't there any other suitable accommodations in Bandits Hollow?"

"Well," Barrett replied, "I could whisk you away to the Iron Feather Brothers Ranch." He looped his thumbs into his front pockets and mulled it over. "But my brother Lander would try to hit on you all night. He's relentless."

Lainey giggled. "I think I can hold my own, Officer Iron Feather," she sassed back. "I'm pretty good with a rifle these days. On film, anyway."

Barrett narrowed his eyes. "Aren't you the same woman I rescued from a creepy reality show star a few hours ago? As I recall, I had to throw him off the set."

"Oh yeah," Lainey replied, biting her lip. "That did get awkward, huh?"

"Actually, I know of a pretty special place for tonight, if you're up for it," Barrett offered. "But it will involve riding horses again."

"As long as there are *no* ghosts or ancestors, or whatever you want to call them," she replied adamantly. "I don't think my heart rate could handle that again. Okay?"

Barrett appeared mildly amused, as though to him such experiences weren't entirely unusual. "Well, I can't promise anything when it comes to being around the Iron Feather brothers," he admitted. "We *are* descended from a renowned medicine man."

"Great," Lainey responded. "How on earth do you guys get any sleep? Can't you put a *Closed* sign in the window for that kind of thing?"

Barrett tilted his head as though appraising Lainey from the inside out, making her fidget. "Lainey, if I *I'm* with you," he assured her thoughtfully, "I don't think there'll be much of a reason for...contact...again. I noticed nothing more happened last night once I arrived to make sure you were safe."

"Thank God," Lainey said in relief, hoping his words were true. "And you promise to stick by my side, right?"

"That I can *definitely* promise," Barrett agreed. "C'mon, I think Cinnamon could use a break from Bandits Hollow, too."

Barrett walked with Lainey over to a temporary corral set

up by the movie crew where Sand and Cinnamon were tied to a railing. For a moment, Barrett disappeared into one of the film's tack trailers. When he resurfaced, he was carrying two sleeping bags and camping pillows, which he tied to the back of the horses' saddles.

"An outdoor overnight—with sleeping bags?" Lainey remarked in an unsettled tone. "Looks to me like you've been *planning* this for a while, Barrett," she noted, unsure whether to be impressed or wary. "There won't be any owls around, will there?"

"There'll be everything around—that's why it's called the outdoors," Barrett confirmed, hardly easing her nerves. "And as for planning," a mischievous smile curled his lip, "guilty as charged. But one thing you won't have is any jerks from Hollywood around to bother you. Sound fun?" His eyes glinted at the thought of taking her on an adventure. "I promise we can come back if you don't like it."

"Do cell phones work out there?" Lainey asked hesitantly, checking her phone to see if she had a signal.

"Sometimes," Barrett replied, "if you manage to find the right ridge." He dug into his pocket and lifted up his cell. "My work mobile phone would get reception on the moon, if that makes you feel any better."

Lainey sucked in a deep breath, weighing her options. "All right, then let's just treat this as a test drive," she bartered, stepping over to grab Cinnamon's reins. She was glad she'd already put on a pair of jeans and t-shirt with a jacket over it in the film trailer, so an assistant could have her costume cleaned. "But if I'm not comfortable," she insisted, "I'm riding straight back to Bandits Hollow before it gets dark. Deal?"

"Deal," Barrett nodded in affirmation.

"Lead the way, cowboy," she said. "And by the way, there had better be some decent chow involved. Because if you try to make me to eat re-constituted, freeze-dried casserole over a campfire, like most people do on camping trips, you're in big trouble."

Although Lainey's tummy began growling, she was pleasantly surprised that the ride wasn't nearly as long as it had been when they went to the Iron Feather Brothers Ranch. In fact, after only twenty minutes, she got the feeling that she recognized this trail. Somewhere in the corners of her memory, she recalled this high-elevation meadow sprinkled by wildflowers, with rolling hills nearby covered in pines. Beyond the hills were the towering peaks of the Rocky Mountains looming over the valley as the trail meandered past an old, rusted plow, long abandoned by pioneers. When they finally came across a weathered barn, Lainey pulled up Cinnamon and stared at the structure, blinking her eyes.

"Wait a minute," she said softly, standing in her stirrups to see get a better view. "We're near where the horse camp used to be, right? This barn," she recollected, "it's the one we used to sneak out to at night—where we'd talk for hours!"

A wistful look arose in Lainey's eyes, and she sank back into the saddle, smiling at the barn as though reconnecting with an old friend. "Those nights we slipped away from camp —that was the only time in my entire childhood I ever got a break from my dad," she confessed softly. She turned to Barrett. "You did that for me."

Barrett met her gaze, noting the sweet reminiscence in Lainey's eyes. "I…I thought you might enjoy coming back here," he said tenderly. "Come on—I brought halters, so we can let the horses graze while we check out the barn. Who knows, there might still be haystack in there. We could climb the ladder to the loft," he smiled at the memory, "and swing from the old rope, like we used to."

"Oh my gosh, I remember!" Lainey gushed, clutching her heart. "That was the most fun I'd ever had in my life! Barrett," she said, speechless for a moment, "it's so thoughtful of you to remember this place. To remember…*us.*"

The expression Lainey caught on Barrett's face made her breath hitch—

There was that burning star again in his eyes—with a heart so bright and pure that longed for her in a way she'd never seen in any other man before. If she didn't know better, she'd call it…

Love.

Lainey shook her head for a second. Could Barrett's ancestor Iron Feather possibly have been right? Did Barrett… *still*…love her?

When Lainey glanced up again at the old barn, it hit her—

He really *did* plan this outing ahead of time, she thought. Based on a sweet memory he never forgot. Couldn't forget—

Just like her?

Lainey's heart did flip flops as a shiver worked its way through her body. Then why didn't his supposed letters ever arrive after all these years, she warred inside, thoroughly confused. Was he making their so-called "connection" now more than it really was? Part of her wanted to believe that— wanted to pretend he was like all of the other shallow guys who got a little infatuated by her Hollywood ties.

But her heart told her she was wrong.

Near as she could tell, Barrett *did* remember—

He remembered everything…

Trying to keep her heart in check, Lainey dismounted from her saddle and untied the leather strap on the cinch, pulling the gear from Cinnamon's back. When Barrett handed her a halter, she threw the rope around the mare's neck and removed the bridle, slipping the halter over her horse's head and buckling it. Then she shot a glance at Barrett, who'd done the same and attached Sand's halter lead to a picket stake in the ground so his horse could freely graze. He came over to Cinnamon and drove in another picket stake with his boot so the mare could graze as well.

"Ready to check out the barn and then have some chow?" he asked.

Lainey scanned the meadow, unable to spy a fire pit anywhere for a cookout. She shrugged. "Sure, but where are we going to cook dinner? Did you bring meat or jerky or something? I didn't see you pack pots or pans—"

"Nope," replied Barrett, taking her gently by the hand. He began to lead her toward the barn, which left Lainey a little anxious.

"Barrett," she said after they'd walked a few strides and reached the barn door, "I hate to break the news to you, but I could eat one of our horses right now. Can we save the rope swinging for after dinner?"

"Not if it *includes* dinner," he smiled slightly, shoving open the barn door.

To Lainey's astonishment, in the middle of the barn was a rustic table with a linen runner down the center and two candelabras on either side, their golden flames flickering. A crystal vase filled with roses was the centerpiece, flanked by silver serving domes and two sets of fine china and silverware. On either side of the table were two vintage wooden chairs. Lainey stood, frozen, when she thought she heard a strain of music…

A lovely classical melody was coming from somewhere behind a stack of hay bales.

The scene was utterly breathtaking.

"Oh Barrett," Lainey gasped, at a loss for words.

"Welcome to Chez Iron Feather," Barrett grinned, leading her toward the table. "I hope you weren't expecting good ol' western chow, like at Nell's restaurant. Because tonight we have," he walked over to one of the serving domes and lifted the lid, "Châteaubriand with roasted vegetables and sautéed mushrooms Provençal for the main course. And over here," he lifted another dome, "we have a side dish of French onion soup topped with Gruyère cheese and baguettes on the side. And finally," he lifted the last dome, "for dessert we have a chocolate soufflé." He nodded at the bottle in the center of the table. "Along with a bottle of Bordeaux. Chateau Latour, of course."

"B-Barrett," Lainey burst in wonderment, "I hardly know what to say!"

"You're not supposed to say anything," he teased. "Sit down and eat!"

He pulled out one of the chairs for Lainey and she sat down, gazing at the delicious spread in front of them. Barrett seated himself across the table, his eyes narrowing.

"I don't want to hear a single word about getting fat tonight," he warned. "If anything, you look like you've dropped a few pounds from the stress of filming lately. So for God's sake," he twisted a corkscrew into the Bordeaux and deftly yanked out the cork, "eat up!"

Lainey giggled, scanning all the food. "Where do I start?"

"Anywhere you damn well please," Barrett replied, pouring them both wine into crystal goblets. He handed one to her and held up his glass for a toast.

"To *Skystone Canyon*," he said, his eyes twinkling as he clinked his glass against hers, "and to the girl who always believes. No matter what."

After taking a sip, Barrett carved slices of meat for himself and Lainey and set them on their plates, turning to serve them vegetables as well. Then he handed her a soup bowl topped with cheese and began to dive into his meal with relish—and no rules. Lainey chuckled inside at the haphazard way he barreled through his Chateaubriand, soup, baguette, and even the soufflé, chomping greedily as though he'd just gotten back from a cattle drive. Enjoying his lack of self-consciousness, she decided to follow suit after eating a few bites of her main course. She skipped the vegetables and soup and boldly dipped her spoon into the chocolate soufflé.

"This is heaven," she moaned in ecstasy, "pure heaven!" She chewed slowly, relishing the rich chocolate on her lips, and she stared into his eyes. "How on earth did you get all this food here? I don't recall seeing tire tracks near the barn."

"That's because there weren't any." Barrett smiled, as though proud of his secret.

Lainey searched her mind for possibilities, her thoughts drifting back to the time she saw the Iron Feather Brothers Ranch. She remembered that they had an airstrip for the Queen, including what looked like a circular, helicopter landing pad—

"Did you have dinner *flown* here?" she asked, astounded at the thought.

Barrett shrugged, his mouth lifting in a smirk. "Beats fighting with Lander all night over you."

Lainey fell silent for a moment, a blush of flattery settling into her cheeks. In all her life, this was the single, most elegant and thoughtful dinner she'd ever seen—glitzy Hollywood parties be damned. She set down her fork and met Barrett's gaze from across the table.

"I don't think you have to worry about any competition," she assured him. "You may not have figured it out yet, Barrett, but I'm actually pretty loyal."

"Oh?" he replied, his voice tinged with challenge.

Lainey nodded resolutely and lifted her chin. "As I recall," she peered past his shoulder to a nearby hay stack, "right over there is where you gave a lonely, chubby girl her first kiss."

Barrett stopped chewing. The way his large brown eyes poured into hers, just like they had on that fateful night all those years ago, told her he hadn't forgotten at all.

In fact, she could tell he'd remembered every detail—

Silence fell between them, so thick that Lainey felt like she could carve it with the meat knife. She straightened in her

chair and removed the linen napkin on her lap, folding it
neatly and setting it on the table.

"To be honest," Lainey confessed, "back then what I
wanted most in the whole wide world was to run away with
you, Barrett Iron Feather." She cleared her throat, pausing for
a second to carefully examine her thoughts. "But I've grown
up a lot since then. I don't try to run away from my problems
anymore. I face them head on, like you taught me that
summer. And I'm a woman of the world now, Barrett. I've
changed—"

"You have?" he said, putting down his knife and fork.
Despite the raw look of yearning in his eyes that made his jaw
slice back and forth, a quiet resignation surfaced on his face, as
if he were stoically accepting his fate.

Lainey slowly stood to her feet and blew out the candles. In
the darkened barn, with only the sunset's glow streaming
through a high window that glinted off the silver, she noticed
that Barrett was far too much of a gentleman to take
advantage of her in this remote setting.

But as far as she was concerned, it was high time to let
etiquette be damned—

Lainey swept off the fine china and silver from the table in
one fell swoop, enjoying the astonishment in Barrett's eyes. She
boldly reached over the table and clutched him by the collar
for a mad kiss.

"Now," she said breathlessly, "all I want is *you*—"

Barrett crawled onto the table and yanked her on top of
him with a brute strength that made her breath catch, pulling
off her shirt and unbuttoning her jeans to wriggle them from
her hips. Then he stripped off his own clothes in a matter of

seconds. He carefully unclasped her bra, pausing to take in the round beauty of her breasts, now allowed full freedom in the open air. The immense hunger in Barrett's eyes overwhelmed Lainey, and the sight of his tan, unbelievably-muscled body set her nerve endings on fire. She pressed her chest tighter to his, cherishing the warm feel of their skin on skin.

"Hold on a second—that's an order," Barrett breathed into her ear as he reached over to his discarded jeans on the table and pulled out a condom, applying it to himself. He rolled on top of her and smothered her in a kiss.

"Officer Iron Feather!" Lainey complained tartly, smoothing her hands with relish against his hard chest and kissing his skin. "That is the very last order I will *ever* tolerate from you."

Barrett laughed. He hesitated for a moment to simply admire her beautiful face, her sky blue eyes. Then he kissed her hard—kissed her as if their lips had the power to transport them both back through time. To that very first moment when their hearts were raw and pure, when they had shared their magical, first kiss. As Barrett broke away, he looked into Lainey eyes like she was indeed the sky that covered his whole world.

Lainey couldn't help falling into his gaze, watching as his deep brown eyes roamed over her face, her neck, her breasts, appreciating every inch of her as they followed down to her navel and thighs. She traced the toned muscles on his abdomen with her palms, marveling at the way the mere touch of him ignited sparks deep in her core. Lainey's body ached for Barrett, and she grabbed his penis and greedily pressed him inside her.

Talk about the sun—

His first thrusts sent her body ablaze as he leaned forward and circled her nipples with his tongue, one after the other, driving her crazy. His slow, smooth movements, artfully swiveling inside her to maximize her pleasure, sent Lainey reeling. She clutched at his firm buttocks, then raced her hands up and down his tight, muscular back, finally grabbing at his thick hair when his deep and slow penetrations started to drive her over the brink. At that moment, he dipped his hand to her wet folds and pulsed his finger on just the right spot, sending her body into ripples of pleasure.

"Barrett!" she gasped, feeling completely out of control, her body burning in ecstasy. Barrett sucked on her breasts again, moving skillfully inside her so that every surface of pleasure would be ignited. "Barrett!" she moaned between swirling throbs of mind-blowing rapture. "I'm-I'm coming. Come with me," she demanded. "That's an order!"

Barrett smiled at her irony, enjoying her complete surrender to abandon and the way her hands seized his buttocks again with all her might to pull him in harder. He buried his fingers in her long, tangled hair, and then claimed her lips—claimed all of her—as he drove against her with such power that for a moment they both felt like the barn had burst into flames.

Gently, Barrett let himself relax onto Lainey's trembling body and slipped his arms around her to hold her tight. He buried his face into her long hair and tenderly stroked her cheek.

"I've waited ten years for you, Lainey," he whispered. "*All* of you."

To Barrett's surprise, she rolled on top of him, her eyes creased with questions.

"Ten years? Then why…" her voice trailed off, the pain of their lack of connection over the last decade cinching at throat.

"What?" Barrett said, concerned. He sat up, lifting her onto his lap. "What is it, Lainey?"

"W-why didn't your letters ever reach me," she asked, her voice trembling at the rawness of how much it really meant to her. "I was crazy about you Barrett—I wrote to you for years, even when I got nothing back." Shaking her head, she tried to will her eyes not to mist at the edges.

"Lainey," Barrett assured her softly, "somewhere in the world out there are the hundreds of letters I wrote to you, burning a hole down to the center of the earth. I don't know why they never reached you. But I do know," he paused and gazed into her eyes, "that they kept…my dream…alive."

"Dream? What dream?"

Barrett cupped her cheeks, his face filled with such intense yearning for the woman he loved that it made her tremble. "My dream that one day, you'd finally…be…*mine*."

The ardent way he said "mine," followed by a kiss that seized her by the heart, made butterflies swirl in Lainey's stomach. He bowed his forehead against hers.

"Today," Barrett whispered, "my dream came true."

He lifted up her hand and entwined his fingers in hers, bringing them to his lips for a kiss. In the sunset glow of the barn, he gazed at their knuckles, wincing when he observed their similar scars.

Lainey felt a shiver course through his strong, hard body that fit like a glove next to hers.

She knew exactly why—

Their souls fit as if they were pieces of the same puzzle. Part pain, part loss, part love, part…

Loyalty.

"Barrett," Lainey whispered as she raised her finger to softly outline his lips. She gave him another soft kiss. "Do you ever wish you and I could have somehow met without all of these scars?" She gazed at the marks on their knuckles in the thin light.

"No," he replied, shaking his head. He stared into her eyes. "They're what make us….*us*."

Lainey smiled. "Barrett Iron Feather, that has to be the wisest thing I've ever heard a man say. And next time," she smoothed her hand over his cheek, "I'm not going to make you wait another ten years. Now let's put on our clothes, cowboy." She glanced at a long rope that hung from the ceiling beside the barn loft. "So we can jump into that old haystack over there before we run out of light. I've waited a helluva long time to roll with my favorite cowboy in the hay."

"What the HELL?!"

The sound of Harper Stone's booming voice echoed across the set the following afternoon, causing the cattle to sound off in a nearby pasture and encouraging everyone in the crew run for cover. Her indignant outburst was followed by a blue streak of curses that made even the most seasoned equipment roadies blush. Lainey sat on a folding chair next to Deb after they'd finishing filming for the day and she'd changed clothes, fearing the earth might start rumbling beneath their feet. The two women watched Harper pace back and forth in front of the storyboard easel, gesturing with her hands and biting the head off of whoever was on the other end of the line.

"There she blows," whispered Deb, shaking her head. "I don't envy the person on the phone with her."

"Geez, I've seen her upset before, but this beats all,"

replied Lainey. "Luckily, we only have a few more scenes left. Hope whatever it is, it's something that can be fixed."

Deb patted Lainey's knee. "Knowing Harper," she said, "heads will roll if anything tries to get in her way."

To the women's astonishment, they saw Harper throw her phone down on the ground and stomp it with her high heel. When that didn't do enough damage, she stormed toward an equipment trailer and returned with a hammer. Setting her phone on a table, she began to beat it to pieces.

A few yards away, Barrett dropped the reins for his horse Sand to ground tie and dismounted, sauntering toward Lainey and Deb. He shot a glance at Harper.

"In the words of the immortal John Wayne," he said, watching Harper take her last hammer swing at the phone, "she reminds me of me."

"I've never seen her like this," fretted Lainey. "Everyone knows she's got a temper, but this is epic."

When Harper was done destroying her phone, she turned and carefully straightened her black blazer and smoothed back her hair, collecting herself to appear once again the Hollywood goddess. With methodical strides, she walked toward the crew and barked at them to come out of their hiding places. Then she sucked in a deep breath and folded her arms.

"*Skystone Canyon* actors and crew," she said in an oddly clipped tone, "it is with a certain degree of unforeseen distress that I must inform you that we—as in, this film project—have lost our funding."

Gasps broke out among the crew, followed by a steady stream of murmurs. Harper held up her palm for silence.

"After Easton Wolfe was...removed...and Cayden Hart departed, one of our investors has decided to back out. The studio just called to let me know of the less than desirable circumstances we currently face."

She scanned the crew members with her dark glasses on, making it impossible to read her emotional state. Then to everyone's surprise, she whipped them off and tossed them toward her broken cell phone, setting her hands on her hips.

"I'm standing here to inform everyone today," she said in a deeply determined tone, "that I am going to move heaven and earth to finish this film, even if I have to go personally bankrupt in the effort. So if you can bear with me, I intend to look at the dailies with our film editor right now," she nodded at a man to her right, "to see if we can create a promo reel to market to other investors. It may take some time, and I'm sincerely asking you for your patience while we continue to pursue funding—"

"What do we do in the mean time?" piped up one of the grips in front of her. "This changes the scheduling and everything, right?"

"What you *do*," Harper said in a low growl, "is decide right here and now how important this film is to your heart. If *Skystone Canyon* means anything to you, I suggest you get off your ass and start praying for a miracle—"

"That won't be necessary," Barrett cut in, to everyone's surprise. "I know some investors who might be interested in this project." He scanned the rest of the crew. "But we won't be able to give you an answer until tomorrow morning. Which means for right now, you are all excused for the rest of the evening."

Harper's mouth dropped as though Barrett had slapped her in the face. Despite his vaguely positive remarks, she was clearly unaccustomed to anyone pulling the rug of control from beneath her sky-high heels. Harper's hands folded into fists, and she began marching toward Barrett.

"I don't give a damn whether you're a cop or how alpha cowboy you are," she spit out, fuming at the way the crew members were already gathering up their things for the day. "*No one* tells my crew what to do or where to go without my permission. Got that? I'm going to call your police chief right away and give him a piece of my mind—"

"On what? Those remnants of your cell phone that fell to the grass? Hope you have tweezers, because it's going to take quite a while to try to put all that back together. And for your information, Miss Stone, I suggest you sweeten your approach by about a mile. Because *I am* one of your potential investors."

Harper stood still in shock.

"Follow me, and don't ask too many questions." He extended his hand out to Lainey so she would rise from her chair to her feet. "Because Miss Lainey Neil is about to give the performance of her life."

Within minutes, a gale wind descended on the pasture adjacent to the *Skystone Canyon* equipment area, nearly knocking Harper and Lainey down. Barrett was already crouched on his heels as soon as he spied the helicopter about to descend. "Get down," he hollered his instructions to the women, "till they open the door and I tell you to run."

Lainey turned to Deb and gave her a hug.

"Knock 'em dead, honey!" Deb cheered her on, gazing into Lainey's eyes. "Show 'em what you're made of."

"Thank you," Lainey replied, gripping her hand. She felt Barrett's arm around her shoulder, encouraging her to head for the helicopter.

"Time to hustle, ladies!" Barrett commanded as he led the dash for the helicopter.

As soon as they reached the landing pad, Lainey looked up and realized that the helicopter had *Iron Feather Brothers Enterprises* emblazoned on its side above the feather brand logo. Barrett ushered Lainey and Harper to ascend the mobile stairsteps and helped them inside to their seats, then closed the large door.

"Ladies, meet Roger, our pilot," he said. "He's done several tours of Afghanistan and worked for our last president, so you have nothing to worry about," Barrett assured them, patting Roger on the shoulder. "Time to relax and enjoy the view."

View is right! Lainey thought, her heart hammering as fast as a hummingbird's. Despite her trepidation at never having ridden in a helicopter before, she couldn't deny that as soon as they ascended, the vista was stunning. The large windows gave them a spectacular view of the rugged Rocky Mountains, filled with deep green forests of pine and aspen. She had to admit, it felt strange to be here on "Hollywood business," when the scenery below her made her feel as far away from Los Angeles as humanly possible. For years, her life had been a concrete jungle of hustling to auditions on clogged highways and living in crummy, month-to-month apartments, and now she was in…

Paradise.

It wasn't until Barrett pointed out the Iron Feather Brothers Ranch, however, that Lainey clutched her chest at the striking beauty.

Below her was the full grandeur of their spread, marked by the fabulous, two-story main ranch house and matching guest buildings. But from this perspective, she also saw that the ranch had an Olympic-size swimming pool and an equestrian center with indoor and outdoor arenas, plus a shooting range, and a river running through the property that was occupied by a couple of fly fisherman. About a half a mile away was the air strip and helicopter landing pad, with a fleet of vehicles prepared to take guests to their appropriate locations.

Roger aimed for the landing pad and gently landed the helicopter, cutting the engine while Barrett opened the door and set out the mobile stairsteps for Harper and Lainey.

"Okay ladies, follow me," he said, taking them by their hands and helping them down. Then he gave Roger a nod. "See you tonight for dinner, buddy?"

"You bet," Roger replied.

Barrett proceeded to walk toward a Hummer with the Iron Feather Brothers logo and invited the women to step in. "Hold on!" he grinned, buckling his seat belt and pulling out his cell phone.

"Lander?" he said, when his brother picked up. "Look, I got an investment opportunity for you, and I'm bringing some people by the house who'd like to pitch it. Is Dillon there?

Good. Because I'm going to need a yes or no answer right away."

To Lainey's and Harper's surprise, Barrett rolled his eyes at the phone and sighed. "Yes, Lander. As a matter of fact, the people pitching this project happen to be women who are spectacularly beautiful. But *hands off*, or you're going to have to deal with me. Got that, bro? Good—I'll see you in a few minutes."

Barrett sighed and tucked his mobile phone back into his jeans. "Lander only has one thing on his brain, ladies," he explained. "And unfortunately, I have to get the signature of both my brothers to authorize funding, so I'm afraid you'll have to put up with him. That doesn't mean you need to take any guff, though. Remember all of those fight moves I taught you?" He turned to Lainey. "Be prepared to show Lander a knuckle sandwich to remind him of his manners."

Barrett steered the Hummer around a bend and up a long, gravel driveway, slowing down as he approached the grand main house.

"Here we are," he said, taking a deep breath. He glanced at Harper and Lainey. "I know it might seem quick, but I figure you have about half an hour to sell this film with everything you've got."

Harper smiled a little, unbuttoning her black blazer to reveal a flask in her inside pocket. She unscrewed the lid and threw back a swallow, tightening the cap once again.

"I'm game," she announced, shooting a glance at Lainey. She gave her a nudge with her elbow. "How about you, pioneer girl?"

"Count me in," Lainey replied, grabbing Harper's flask

and downing a shot as well. She wiped off her lips and stared Barrett in the eye. "Let's get a move on," she said with steel determination in her eyes. "It's showtime."

With that, Barrett stepped out to open the Hummer doors for the women, and he escorted them to the mansion's front door.

He didn't need to knock.

Instantly, a butler opened the front door and stood to attention for Barrett. "Good evening, Master Iron Feather," he said. "I see you have guests."

"Yes, James. Dillon and Lander are expecting us. Please tell Francois to prepare dinner for two extra people while we go to the media room to discuss business."

"As you wish," James replied. "Will you be requiring any particular wines or spirits during your business meeting?"

Barrett tossed a glance at Harper. "No, I think we've got that covered." He led the way with long strides into the grand foyer of the mansion that held massive crystal chandeliers and rustic, western decor. On the walls were vintage rifles and military uniforms along with bows and arrows and deerskin war shirts that appeared to be collected from famous battles. Hanging at the top of the central staircase was a huge, framed vintage photo of the Bandits Hollow Gang. Lainey and Harper seemed mesmerized by it.

"Guess my family members have always been... entrepreneurs," Barrett joked. "Come this way to the media room."

He turned a sharp right and went down a hall, past a palatial dining room and ball room that rivaled Versailles. At the end of the hall, he opened a door and ushered Harper and Lainey inside.

In the room were several comfortable-looking leather chairs with two men seated who were smoking cigars. Before them was a large screen. When Lainey and Harper walked toward them, the two men stood up.

"Oh my God, what wonderment is this!" Lander cried, practically slobbering over the sight of Lainey and Harper. "Damn, Barrett—if I'd known you were bringing back this beautiful woman with her stunning friend, I'd have invited you over a lot sooner. Well hello, visions of perfection—I'm Lander Iron Feather and this is my brother Dillon."

Dillon gave them a silent nod, not one to be as easily effusive as his brother.

"Hey guys," Barrett said, offering Lainey and Harper seats. "I've brought Lainey Neil and Harper Stone here today to talk about funding for their historical western film *Skystone Canyon.*"

"Is it gonna make us money?" Lander boldly inserted. "Because frankly, that's why we're in business."

"I think the bigger question is," Barrett noted, "aside from making a profit, what will it do for the Iron Feather Brothers brand?"

Barrett glanced at Lainey, and she instantly knew this was her moment. Barrett could do all the work to bring the horses to water, but he couldn't make them drink. It was time to fight for *Skystone Canyon* with everything she had.

"Integrity…and grit," Lainey said, standing to her feet. "That's what this film is all about. In the tradition of John Ford's *The Searchers* and Clint Eastwood's *The Unforgiven*, this is a film that doesn't gloss over how hard the old West really was. My main character Ada Holdwell is a widow and a rancher who's all alone in the world doing her damndest to…*stay*. She comes from the kind of stock who keep leaving every disaster that befalls them—cattle rustlers, fires, droughts, wars. But Ada has run as far as she can, and she's decided she's not going to run anymore. She's going to make a stand and fight for the life she's come to love, even if it kills her. And frankly Barrett, Dillon, and Lander, I think people *need* more inspiring movies like this—movies that give people *hope*. But you don't have to believe me. She dug into her pocket for her cell phone. Believe the movie itself."

Lainey tapped on her phone until she brought up video footage of *Skystone Canyon* on her screen.

"You have the dailies on your phone?" Barrett said.

Harper nodded, turning to Barrett's brothers. "We watch the digital dailies every afternoon after filming, and I have them sent to Lainey so she can go over them, in case there's anything she thinks needs to be reshot." Harper sent Lainey an appreciative glance. "She has good instincts."

Barrett took the phone from Lainey and held it up to his brothers. "Give me a second, and I'll feed this to our large screen."

As Barrett disappeared through a side door, Lainey inhaled a deep breath and secretly grabbed Harper's hand where the men couldn't see. This was it—the Iron Feather brothers were about to view a scene that she'd poured her whole heart into in order to make their decision. With a lump in her throat, she watched as the lights in the media room grew dim and her image loomed on the screen over ten feet tall. In this scene, she was gazing out over the green pasture at her cattle herd with a rifle in her hand. Her face was dirty and her eyes were filled with more than fatigue—she appeared to be at her last shot for survival. Barrett returned to the chairs beside the women while his brothers stared at the footage.

The character of Ada Holdwell squinted into the camera with sheer venom. She hoisted her rifle into her arms and pointed at someone beyond the frame.

"I know what you're thinkin'," she hissed, her finger steady on the trigger. "You're convinced I'm some dumb tenderfoot who's too stubborn for her own good. When I could be hightailing back to some pretty city and marrying the first man I see to get out of these kinds of troubles. But what you don't know, Mister, is that I got troubles deeper inside my heart than you'll ever know. And I ain't sellin' out so goddamned cheap. One of those troubles is this land you see here. This is *my* land, and it's gonna stay my land. I'm the one who raised those calves out there, bottle feeding the orphaned ones to build up this herd. And that's my corn over in that field that I planted with my own hands. I helped build my log cabin in Skystone Canyon with sweat and blood. So don't you dare think for a second that if there ain't no man around that I'm gonna let you tear my heart out of my chest and allow you to steal this ranch. If you take one measly step closer, you God-forsaken varmint, you'd better say a prayer before I shoot you to pieces. Because I intend to bury you as far as possible from my property in unmarked grave, out in the howling wilderness where not even ghosts will dare to find you."

"Cut! That's enough!" Lander stood and announced as the camera pulled back from Ada Holdwell's face, revealing the cabin and the ranch she held so dear. Barrett got up and slipped into the back room again to freeze the frame, returning to hear what Lander and Dillon had to say. As soon as he sat down in his chair, Lander walked up to high-five Lainey and Harper.

"I don't know about Dillon and Barrett," he said, "but from what I just saw, that girl can kick some ass! I think movie audiences will go crazy for her."

Barrett stared at his brother Dillon, trying to read his face, when he saw his lip curl upward a little. Dillon pointed to a large ponderosa tree to the right of Ada Holdwell in the frame. "Something tells me Iron Feather would approve," he said cryptically.

Puzzled, the others got up and walked closer to the screen, peering at the tree.

There, on a branch, was a great horned owl.

Harper shook her head and turned to Lainey. "I don't understand," she whispered.

"It's okay," Lainey replied, barely able to speak after getting choked up from what she'd seen. She snuck a glance at the owl again and linked her arm through Harper's. "I think it means they're going to fund our film. Now, for the love of God, hand me the flask in your jacket pocket, before I pass out."

After Lander and Dillon agreed to talk with Harper about the logistics for funding *Skystone Canyon*, Barrett slipped away and escorted Lainey to an elevator to take her to her guestroom on the second floor. When the elevator doors opened, to her astonishment, he picked her up in his arms.

"I believe you've gotten tipsy from Harper's Bourbon," Barrett said. "Wouldn't want you to turn an ankle on the way to your room. After earning a reputation as Apollo 13, that's the last thing *Skystone Canyon* needs. Besides," he headed down the hall with her in his arms and carefully set her on her feet to open her door, "you didn't want to stay in the Golden Wagon Hotel again, did you? I can have dinner delivered to your room."

"Wait a second…" Lainey glanced around the guestroom, luxuriously appointed with rustic leather furniture, a spacious king-size bed, antique Navajo rugs and a river-rock fireplace. Thankfully, there wasn't a taxidermied bear in sight. "This room is fabulous by anyone's measure," she observed. "But if all three of you brothers are descendants of Iron Feather, he has all the more reason to want to hang around here, right?"

She turned to face Barrett. "I think you'd better stay the night with me, cowboy," she giggled, kicking the door closed with her boot. "You know, for *security*." Then she clenched her hands and put them on her hips. "And I'm not nearly as tipsy as you think. In fact, I can balance on one leg." Lainey artfully lifted a foot and remained steady to prove her point. "And I noticed quite clearly that you haven't congratulated me yet on winning over your brothers."

Barrett narrowed his gaze. "That's because I don't trust my brothers with a woman as beautiful as *you* in the house. In case you didn't notice, I whisked you away awfully fast."

"No worries, Officer Iron Feather," she whispered, tossing aside his cowboy hat and unbuttoning his shirt. "I'm not drunk, and I'm no pushover. After all the years I've spent in Hollywood, there's one thing I find more attractive than all the money in the world, and even sexier than your kick-ass body," she smirked, yanking his shirt off and admiring his outrageously toned chest and arms.

"What might that be?" Barrett arched a brow. He worked his fingers over the buttons on Lainey's clothing, flinging aside her shirt and unclasping her bra, letting her firm breasts fall free. Then he simply stood and gazed at her beauty, as though she were a fine treasure that he had to pinch himself to believe was really in the same room with him.

Lainey slipped off her jeans and tossed them aside, then

pulled down Barrett's jeans as well, allowing him to wriggle off his boots. Standing completely naked with him, she linked her arms around his neck and pressed her chest to his, feeling her heart beat fast.

"Loyalty," Lainey whispered. "It's the rarest commodity on earth." The way she let those words roll off her lips in a low tone made the concept sound downright seductive. "Hollywood is filled with beautiful bodies and padded bank accounts. But beautiful souls? They're in short supply. And I must admit, Barrett, along with your rocking body, that makes you pretty much the sexiest man I've ever seen."

Barrett lifted her in his arms, and Lainey wrapped her legs around his waist, relishing the feel of his hot skin. Then he kissed her madly, stepping over to lay her down on the king-size bed.

"Please tell me you have a condom in your jeans pocket, like last time," she said hopefully, gazing up at him.

Barrett stepped over to the wall and flipped a switch to turn on the gas fireplace, which set off his god-like physique and tanned skin with an amber glow. Then he grabbed his jeans and pulled out a condom.

"I was secretly hoping we'd have celebration sex at some point." His lip curled in a half smile. "Believe me, I want to celebrate every hot inch of you." Without another word, he slipped on the condom and began to run his tongue up Lainey's thigh, making her gasp. Gently, he separated her legs and began to pulse her inner folds with his tongue, sending Lainey into a building momentum of pleasure. Grabbing his thick, dark hair, her fingers dug into his scalp as she writhed, stunned that he could artfully arouse her so quickly. Barrett's tongue undulated up and down, then circled her delicately, brushing over her clitoris with just the right amount of pressure and soft strokes until she thought she might explode.

"Not yet, Barrett!" she said, tugging on his shoulders to slide on top of her. She couldn't stop herself—she had to have him inside, to feel his long hardness filling her up to the brim. Greedily, she swallowed him between her legs, feeling the slick thrusts of his flesh make her body soar as he cupped her breasts, stimulating her nipples until they tingled in ecstasy. "Oh Barrett," she whispered as he slowly swiveled his hips to reach every tender place of arousal inside her—some she didn't even know existed.

Barrett turned her over so she was on top of him and began to drink from her breasts, sucking one and then the other, while her hips moved with a rhythm that was driving him wild. "You are *so* beautiful, Lainey," he said, breaking for a moment to stare into her blue eyes. "How did I ever get this lucky?"

"Well, you did invest in my movie," she smiled, pivoting her hips and watching him reel from pleasure. "And as I recall, you let me kiss you on camera." She traced her hands over his six-pack abs, still having trouble believing this was real—that such a gorgeous specimen of masculinity could possibly be flesh and blood and on the bed with her. Barrett rolled over once more so he was on top, and he kissed her fiercely.

"I want to drive you mad," he gasped, thrusting harder as his finger lowered to pulse her clitoris. Lightning bolts of pleasure coursed through Lainey, leaving her shattered yet gasping for more.

"Barrett, come with me—now!" she cried as he drove hard

and deep, lifting her legs at the knees to maximize her pleasure. Smoothly, he pulled in and out, each time sinking himself into Lainey with a force that left her body trembling. His pounding rhythm sent her into explosive spirals, ripping her breath away as she abandoned herself completely to him. When Barrett reached his climax, he gently collapsed on her chest, burying his head in her breasts.

Lainey ran her fingers through his hair, feeling sweat trickle off his forehead. Barrett kissed her between her breasts and slipped his arms beneath her, holding her in silence.

"So this is a...guestroom, huh?" she said, glancing up at the grand elk antler chandelier, then eyeing the antique Native American woven baskets and cowhide chairs. Hanging on the wall was an old bow and a beaded quiver with arrows that looked like they'd seen many battles. "Barrett," she said softly, "how come, throughout the Russian roulette of our lodging options lately, you've never taken me to where _you_ live?"

Barrett hugged her closer, nuzzling into the softness of her skin. "Because I live in the same place I always have," he replied. "Like you said, I guess I'm...loyal." He lifted himself up and perched his hands on either side of her shoulders, staring into her eyes. "I treasure what's important to me, Lainey," he explained, "which includes _you_." His lips lifted in one of those drop-dead gorgeous half smiles. "You might say I'm the kind of guy who's in it for the long haul."

Barrett kissed her long and slow, refreshing the tingles up and down her body. The way he gazed into her eyes left no doubt that when this Iron Feather brother gave his heart, it was for keeps. Still, Lainey had to wonder...

"Then why haven't you shown your place to me?" she

asked, stroking a wayward lock of hair from his eyes. "My life is laid bare to you—you know everything about my career, my dad, and now Deb. You've seen the trailers and horses we use on the set, you've even been in my hotel room. But to me, you're like a dark continent, Barrett. Sure, you brought me to the fancy corporate ranch you share with your brothers," she glanced around again, "but this room is designed for strangers right? I feel like you know all my secrets, but I'm never privy to the deepest parts of you. I mean, after camping in the barn the other day, you already know I'm hardly a snob—and this ranch isn't what impresses me about your life."

Barrett's jaw twisted, and she could feel the muscles in his body tighten against her. For a moment, Lainey's heart began to race, wondering if she'd overestimated the depth of their bond. The second those thoughts ran through her mind, Barrett gave her a kiss, as if he'd sensed her misgivings with an invisible radar dialed into her innermost emotions.

"Lainey," he replied in a husky whisper, as though speaking from a deep sanctuary hidden in his heart, "don't you realize I would have taken you to my place the first minute I saw you again in Bandits Hollow? But I always told myself something —that the woman I finally brought to my childhood home would be the woman I would *never* let go of again. That place is my heart, my soul. And if it's something you want to see," he gazed sharply into her eyes, "you can't be an actress or a tourist. Do you understand? No one who works or comes to our ranch is ever allowed to go there except for the Iron Feather brothers. It's sacred, Lainey." He drew in a long breath, searching her face as though scrutinizing her soul.

"And there's nothing more I want in this world than to take you to my home. But you have to want that, too."

Lainey studied his eyes, and for the first time she truly saw the decade of longing for her pent up there, the kind of admiration that transcended anything she'd ever witnessed from her dad or from Hollywood. Here was a man who made commitments to the people he loved with every ounce of integrity he had to offer.

Was she that kind of person, too?

All of her life she'd floated from job to job, apartment to apartment. But what she saw in Barrett's eyes was real and true...

And Lainey wanted that with every fiber of her being.

She linked her legs around him and kissed him—hard.

"I want *you*, Barrett Iron Feather," she said breathlessly. "Take me to you. Take me to all of you."

❧ 24 ❧

Barrett drove the Hummer without using headlights on a remote stretch of dirt road on the Iron Feather Brothers Ranch, guided only by the moon. After several miles, he approached an old cabin alongside a stream, its ripples glinting in the moonlight. In the darkness, Lainey made out an old corral with a couple of horses and a cattle chute nearby. As the Hummer approached, she heard the horses nicker.

Lainey squinted at the cabin. There were no power lines running to the structure, no lights or signs of neighbors anywhere. The cabin appeared as close to living on the frontier as you could get in the present day. She turned to Barrett.

"This is your house—where you grew up?"

He nodded, listening to a horse's whinny grow louder. "I think someone's happy to see you," he smiled. Lainey lifted in her seat a little, spying a dappled gray mare next to Sand in the corral, their shiny coats illuminated by the moon. Her mind raced back to their horse camp days when the gray horse had been a filly, only six months old. "Storm?" she gasped. "Is that Storm, the filly you taught me horsemanship lessons with?"

Barrett nodded. "When I got older, I bought her from Rick, the camp owner. It was a way of…trying to connect with you…I guess."

"Oh Barrett!" Lainey clutched her heart. "Can I go see her? She must be a little over ten now. Do you think she'll remember me?"

"There's one way to find out," Barrett said, cutting the engine. They stepped out of the Hummer and walked over to the corral, where Barrett pulled a rawhide loop off the gate to let them in. Storm lifted her head, tossing it in air and nickering as if to say hello.

"She's fully grown now—and she's beautiful," gasped Lainey, admiring the way the moon highlighted her silvery dappled hide. "I remember how you taught me to be still in the arena and allow her to be comfortable enough to come up to me, and we gentled her to accept a halter at the camp. You showed me how to lead her around, to clean her hooves and brush her. I…I fell in love with her, Barrett," Lainey smiled, "along with Sand."

"I know," Barrett said. "That's why I couldn't bear not to have her. Do you want to try riding her?"

"Here, without a saddle or a bridle?" Lainey asked nervously.

Barrett gripped her hand—his fingers felt warm and

strong. "You're friends, remember? This isn't your dad's style of horsemanship, where he kept badgering you to dominate the animal. This is more like a…reunion. Here," he handed her a small, looped rope with a feather dangling from it that held two rings and a long, thin leather strap, "this is all you'll need. It's a war bridle—I made it myself. Just approach Storm and slip the loop in her mouth and put the strap over her neck, and you're all set."

"Easier said than done?" Lainey replied, eyeing the bridle warily.

"Not if you feel your way through it. Think back, Lainey," Barrett urged. "Listen to the horse, and follow your heart."

Lainey inhaled a heavy breath, wondering if this was some kind of test. If she could recall the nuances Barrett had taught her about horsemanship—Iron Feather style—would she then be worthy to go inside his cabin? Inside his soul?

"It's all about the relationship," Lainey whispered, reaching far back in her memory. She mulled over her thoughts for a moment and turned to Barrett. "You told me your mother's people were a horse tribe. From an early age, they used to take foals into their teepees. They'd eat with them, stay warm with them, become their brothers and sisters." She glanced into his eyes. "They formed a lifelong bond…a heart connection that endured forever. That's why you said it never does any good to bully animals—you wouldn't dream of doing that to a friend."

Barrett kept silent in the darkness, but Lainey noticed his chest had swelled. She felt proud of herself for calling to mind his words from so long ago, and she quietly took the war bridle and walked towards Storm.

Then she remembered—

When she reached the middle of the corral, she turned her back and waited patiently, allowing Storm to take the initiative and walk up to her from behind. Before long, she felt a warm, moist breath on her shoulder, the velvet nose nibbling at her neck to say hello. Lainey smiled and cautiously swiveled around to breathe into the horse's nostrils her polite greeting while making sure she remained shoulder to shoulder with the horse before running her hand along Storm's warm neck. Each of these comforting maneuvers that Barrett had taught her were designed to telegraph to the horse that she was its *friend*—not a predator ready to attack. Then Lainey slipped her finger into the gap between the horse's teeth and adjusted the rope loop in her mouth, lifting the leather rein over her head. Storm nudged her, as though expecting a ride—some kind of fun adventure. "I think we're just trying this out in the corral," she whispered, afraid she might be disappointing the mare. Lainey drew a deep breath and grabbed a tuft of Storm's mane near the withers and swung her right leg with all her might over the mare's back. Heart pounding, she prayed a soft thank you to the horse gods that she managed to land successfully. After settling in a little, she nudged Storm with her legs and urged the mare to stroll around the corral.

"You did it!" Barrett smiled wide, clearly proud of her. Lainey's heart swelled, realizing as she gazed at the horizon with the snow-capped mountains in the distance that glistened in the moonlight, just like the silvery dapples on Storm's coat, that this might actually be the most beautiful night she'd ever seen. To her astonishment, Barrett slipped onto Storm's back in a flash behind Lainey, and he closed his hands over hers on the reins. "Come on," he said, nudging Storm over to the gate. He lifted the loop off the wood post and opened it. "Let's let Storm have a little fun."

Before Lainey knew it, they were galloping in the moonlight. Normally, Lainey would have been petrified to go so fast on a horse without a saddle, but Barrett held her close with one arm while his other was on the reins, their bodies moving in gentle rhythm with the horse, which made her feel completely safe. They galloped across a meadow, everything around them glinting silver like a magical world in the crisp moonlight. Barrett easily turned the horse by simply gripping tighter with his left leg, and they galloped along the stream with platinum ripples flowing past them. Soon, they headed back to the corral, Storm's long mane flying high in the night. Barrett pulled the mare up and gently trotted her inside, where he brought her to a halt.

"Atta girl, *Gaatkiit*," he said softly, which Lainey presumed meant the mare's name in Apache. Barrett slipped down from the horse and waited for Lainey to do the same. As soon as he removed the war bridle from Storm, Sand came up and bumped Lainey's back from behind. "It's okay, *Saayi*," Barrett whispered, laughing a little. "You'll get your turn next time."

Then Barrett clutched Lainey's hand and squeezed it as she gave Sand a pat. He led her to the old cabin in the moonlight. Opening the door for Lainey, he guided her into its darkness, marked only by a stream of silvery light flowing through a window. Barrett let go of her hand and went over to a dresser, pulling out a matchbook to strike a match. He grasped a hurricane lamp and lit the wick, setting the lamp back on the dresser. The flame created a soft, warm light in the room.

"This is where I grew up," he said. "Without electricity or plumbing. But we had the sun and the moon," he nodded at the silver light from the window. "And the creek that runs all year past this cabin. We also had each other."

Lainey noticed there was only one big bed in the middle of the room with quilts piled on top of it, which she wondered if they'd all shared. Barrett laughed a little.

"My brothers and I slept on the floor," Barrett said, as if reading her thoughts. "With the foals or herding dogs, or whatever we were bonding with at the time."

Lainey nodded, gazing at the walls in the spare one-room cabin. A few bridles hung on a rack, and there were beautiful Navajo rugs on the floor. But with the exception of a photo in a frame on Barrett's dresser, very little adorned the place. Clearly, that's the way he wanted it. Lainey walked over to the photo on the dresser beside the hurricane lamp. She recognized the woman in the frame as Barrett's mother, with a tall blonde man at her side who must have been his father. Three boys stood next to them, smiling in the picture.

"That's my family," Barrett said with a tinge of wistfulness in his voice. "I've never shown anyone else this cabin, Lainey —or that picture."

Barrett closed up behind her. She could feel the warmth of his body as he slipped his arms around her waist. Lainey turned around and kissed him.

"Thank you," she whispered, glancing around the cabin. "For showing me your…soul."

"Sh…" Barrett replied, tipping his forehead against hers.

Then he picked up the hurricane lamp and blew out the flame, setting it down and reaching up his hand to gently stroke a lock of hair away from her temple. He circled his strong arms around her and held her close for a long time, simply pressing his hard jaw against her soft cheek. The way he held her tight made Lainey think he wanted to cherish this moment, with her in his cabin, and somehow seal it in his heart forever.

Then silently, Barrett picked Lainey up and carried her over to the bed, setting her gently down on the soft quilts. Laying beside her, he encased her once again in his arms.

"For tonight," he whispered in her ear, "let's fill the silence with our hearts. And just *be*."

25

A harsh ring startled Lainey from her dream featuring soft images of a midnight ride under moonlight in the arms of a handsome cowboy. Irritated by the interruption, she flicked open her eyes, spying Barrett on his work phone beside her in the bed. The early morning light cast a warm glow on the rough-hewn logs of the cabin and highlighted the rich hues of the Navajo rugs. From the way the sunlight slanted through the window, Lainey guessed it must be barely past dawn, and she rubbed her eyes, wondering what merited a work call at this hour. She sat up in bed, gazing at Barrett.

"Got it," he said with a serious look on his face. "I'll be there right away."

He clicked off the phone and turned to Lainey. "There's been a…fire," he stated ominously. "At the Skystone Canyon cabin, where you're supposed to film your final scene."

Lainey's hand covered her mouth in shock.

"It's okay," he assured her, "smoke was spotted rising from the canyon not long ago, and the fire department called Lander for support. He authorized Roger to fly the helicopter to the river nearby and drop buckets of water on the cabin to put it out."

"Oh, thank God," Lainey said, relieved. She gripped Barrett's arm. "That old cabin is beautiful—was there much damage?"

Barrett shook his head. "No, only a corner of it was burned, facing the river. But the thing is," he pointed at the gorgeous blue sky outside the window, "there isn't a single cloud outside this morning, Lainey—no reason for lightning to strike and start a fire."

A chill went up Lainey's back. "What are you saying? More confirmation that this film is Apollo 13, like the other mishaps on the set?"

Barrett stared into her eyes. "Guess it's my job to determine that. But it doesn't look good." He pulled off the covers and threw on his jeans and shirt. "Come on, we have an investigation to do. Then I promise to grab you some breakfast."

When Barrett and Lainey reached the cabin deep in the canyon, smoke was still rising from the corner that faced the river.

With a granite expression, Barrett cut the engine and stepped out of his Hummer in full work mode. He walked over to the blackened corner of the cabin and began to take pictures of the charred wood and the ground beside it. Then he pulled out a jackknife and collected samples of the burnt wood and soil, slipping them into separate ziplock bags. To Lainey's surprise, he poked his nose into the cabin's logs and chinking to inhale a deep whiff, then held up his camera to snap more photos. When he was finished, he walked over to the front of the cabin and peered inside a window. He made an attempt to open the door, but it was locked.

"Who has the key to the cabin right now?" Barrett asked Lainey. "There's a can of kerosene in there, the same fuel used as an accelerant on the wood—the smell is unmistakable. This is a case of arson, and whoever set the flame probably got it from inside, so it couldn't be traced to a store."

"A-Arson?" Lainey replied, shocked. "I know Harper has a couple of keys, because the set technicians went inside yesterday to make sure everything would be perfect for today's final scene. They told me she got the keys from the Mayor, and she regulates them like gold. Other than her, I don't know who else would have any."

"Except for Easton Wolf," Barrett commented, "but he was dragged off to jail. The county will keep his personal articles locked up till he gets his hearing, so that rules him out. Is there any reason Cayden Hart would have had a key?"

Lainey mulled it over. "Come to think of it, he dragged the lighting technicians with him down here early on during filming because he wanted his close-ups to be perfect." She rolled her eyes. "Predictable, right? He could have swiped a key from them before Harper even started directing. But why would he hang onto it and sabotage a film he'd *left?*"

Barrett arched a brow. "To prove it was never going to hit the market anyway. Maybe he hated the project all along, and he didn't want to look like a quitter."

Lainey's pulse raced—could a saboteur like him be right under their nose, still somewhere in Bandits Hollow? How could Barrett prove that?"

Barrett pulled out his camera again and took a picture of the soil near the door, then pointed at a footprint on the ground. "Know anybody who has big feet, with tread that might match this?"

Lainey squinted at the clear footprint evident beside the cabin. It looked like a man's shoe size, and there was a distinct impression of the word *Gucci* in the center. She shook her head and shrugged.

"The air's so dry here at nine-thousand feet, even a cigarette butt could have caused this fire, right?" she said. "Maybe somebody simply spilled the kerosene before putting it in the cabin, and there was a smoker nearby."

"Well, you're right about the smoker," Barrett replied, spying an unusual black and gold cigarette butt wedged between blades of grass near the door. He slipped on gloves and picked it up, putting it inside a ziplock bag. "This cigarette butt is outstanding for DNA evidence. But whoever *happened* to spill that kerosene managed to soak this entire side of the cabin, too. Luckily, the flames didn't manage to burn beyond the corner before they were put out, unlike what you see in the movies. You can still detect the kerosene smell. Here, take a whiff."

Barrett gestured at a patch of chinking near the door, and

Lainey leaned forward to inhale deeply. Sure enough, there was the distinct odor of vapors clinging to the cabin.

"Someone doesn't want this film to finish, Lainey," Barrett said gravely. "And whoever it is, that person is dangerous."

Lainey inhaled a tense breath. "Good grief, from the crew who were loyal to Easton Wolfe, to Cayden Hart…shoot, even my ex-boyfriend might have wanted to derail this film! On top of that, the Wings Channel could have decided that insurance would pay out more money if *Skystone Canyon* fails than if it releases. Hunting down perpetrators is like looking for a needle in a haystack around here." She sank her hands into her pockets. "At least I know one thing for certain—all that's left is one last kissing scene this morning, and we're outta here."

"Another kissing scene?" Barrett said.

"Yeah," replied Lainey with a smirk. "So we need you to be a stand-in again in about two hours, poor cowboy. But first," she pointed a finger at him, "you promised me breakfast."

Later that morning, after eating blueberry pancakes and bacon catered for the film crew by the Golden Wagon Restaurant, Lainey and Barrett headed back to Skystone Canyon with the cameramen and technicians to film the final scene. This time, however, the area was surrounded by cameras on dollies, lighting equipment, sound equipment and a small army of film workers who were not allowed to go within twenty feet of the cabin or the evidence Barrett had photographed. Though Lainey's yellow calico dress had been washed in preparation, Lainey leaned down and dipped her hand in the dirt, smudging her dress in a few places so she would still make a convincing homesteader.

"Authenticity," she remarked, smiling at Barrett. "It means everything."

Barrett looked down at his clothing, noting that he never really had to alter himself for the film—western clothing was his daywear. "I don't know what you're talking about," he winked as Harper barked for them to hit their marks. "Ready to wrap this up, Ada Holdwell?"

Lainey nodded, her eyes a bit misty. "This is my first truly adult role," she whispered to Barrett. "I'll never forget this experience."

Barrett linked his arm through hers. "Then let's go out with a bang."

The two of them walked to the red Xs painted on the grass in front of the cabin. A technician fired up a wind machine so Lainey's honey-blonde hair would blow gracefully off her face during the scene. Barrett had to sink his black cowboy hat lower on his head to keep it from whisking away.

"What's next, candles and mood music?" Barrett joked, until Lainey hit him.

"Cut it out," she chided. "This is a big deal to movie audiences. We have to get this right."

"Okay!" Harper called, holding up the script. "At this point in the story, Ned Proctor has been there for Ada Holdwell during cattle raids, torrential rains, a river flood, and a stampede." When the rest of the crew gasped at that information, Harper copped to the truth. "Hell, you'd better believe I ordered a camera to roll during that cattle incident," she stated unapologetically. "Why waste a good disaster?" Her crimson lips curled into a smile. "Lord knows, we've had our share on this film, oddly paralleling Ada Holdwell's life. But now this couple has made it through the hard times," Harper glanced up, "and it's pure blue skies ahead. So please, have the cowboy stand with his back to the camera, and aim the lens over his shoulder to Lainey's face as we shoot this final scene. Mister Cowboy Cop will say his short lines of dialogue from a three-by-five card." Harper nodded to an assistant to give Barrett the cheat card, which would be hidden from the camera's view. "Then I want them to kiss while the dollies pull back to capture the entire landscape, like footage straight out of a John Ford western. Got it?"

The cameraman and technicians saluted Harper while an assistant slammed the clapstick to begin filming the scene.

Barrett glanced down at the two corny lines of dialogue in his hand, straight out of an old-fashioned dime novel, which had Ned Proctor praising himself for his own bravery and pressuring Ada Holdwell to be his woman. He boldly crumpled the card in his hand and tucked it in his pocket. Then he grasped Lainey by the temples and peered into her eyes. Going completely against the script, he brushed a strand of hair from her face and looked at Lainey like she was his entire world.

"Ada Holdwell," he stated in a deep, husky voice, "you are the strongest, most determined woman I've ever seen. As beautiful as you are, it doesn't even compare to the gold in your soul. A gold that's been tried by fire. Look at this land, Ada," Barrett swept his arm to indicate the ranch, "all of this bounty is the work of your hands, and you've defended it with your lifeblood. If there's anyone who deserves the title to the most beautiful place on earth, it's you. I've only played a small part in wars that you were destined to win anyway. And what I want to know, Ada, is this: do you have room in your paradise for me?"

Tears streamed down Lainey's cheeks as she choked up a little. She tilted her head and gazed into Barrett's eyes, before drawing her gaze up to the sky.

"Well, Ned Proctor," she smiled, lifting off his hat, "aside from a few rounds of ammunition you owe me, I do believe the blue sky above Skystone Canyon might just be big enough for both of us."

With that, Barrett seized Lainey for a kiss, wrapping his arms around her tightly as the cameras pulled back. After a few seconds, Harper was supposed to yell cut, but she didn't dare. She kept the cameras rolling as Barrett scooped Lainey in his arms and kissed her even harder. Just before they broke free, Harper sliced her hand in the air to terminate filming, and then simply folded her arms and smiled.

"Lord have mercy!" she cried, her face beaming with pride, even behind her dark sunglasses. "Now *that*, my friends, is how you end a western."

On the grandstand in Memorial Park at twilight, a local band fired up their instruments and began to play a sweet country tune while the smell of barbeque gently wafted over the town of Bandits Hollow. No longer were there any trailers parked at the end of Main Street once the crew had packed up most of the equipment after the completion of the final scene. For once, the *Skystone Canyon* crew had time to relax and enjoy a job well done, despite all the odds.

Strings of outdoor lights hung from the grandstand to nearby lampposts, creating a magical, twinkling canopy for those who wanted to dance as the sun set on the horizon. All the while, the Golden Wagon Restaurant had set out buffet-style tables of barbeque ribs and potatoes with all the fixings, paid for by Harper Stone to thank her loyal crew. When the old-fashioned dinner bell was sounded in Memorial Park, the band stopped playing for a moment. Harper surprised everyone by opening a case of alcohol—not of Bourbon this time, but of champagne. She pulled out a bottle and popped the cork with a big smile on her face as she began to pour its contents into red Solo cups. Then she instructed a couple of the film assistants to pass out the champagne while she picked up a microphone and lifted her cup to the crowd.

"I'd like to make a toast to the best film crew on earth!" she announced, wearing her bright red rodeo shirt and jeans once again, like she had in the bar. "Most crews would have mutinied in the middle of this project, after everything we've been through. And don't think for a second that I haven't recommended each and every one of you for a raise from the Wings Channel. Speaking of Wings, I sent them a digital copy of the unedited film this afternoon, and they were so impressed that…"

Harper paused dramatically, waiting for everyone on picnic blankets on the lawn to stop what they were doing and pay attention. When she was certain she had their sole focus, she lifted the microphone once again to her lips.

"The Wings Channel has decided to turn *Skystone Canyon* into an ongoing, streamed TV series. With yours truly as the director!"

A roar of applause issued from the crowd as everyone rose to their feet to give Harper a standing ovation.

Harper held up her hands to subdue the noise. "This means that if you're interested in continuing with *Skystone Canyon*, you may want to look for a more permanent residence! After all, if the first season of the series becomes a hit, subsequent seasons could go on for years. And aside from that bit of good news, don't forget that after the barbeque dinner tonight, we'll be offering fresh red velvet cake for dessert."

"Did you hear that, Barrett? squealed Lainey. "The Wings Channel wants to develop *Skystone Canyon* into a series!" Unable to contain herself, she threw her arms around him in a hug.

"Congratulations, Lainey," he said, closing his arms tightly. Then he searched her eyes. "So you might become a rather… permanent fixture…in town, eh? Time to go scouting for a new residence?"

"What about you?" she teased. "As I recall, you ended up in more scenes than Cayden Hart."

"You mean my butt did—everything was shot from behind, remember?"

Lainey shrugged. "That's okay. That's all female audiences care about, anyway," she remarked with a wicked gleam in her eye. "It is your best asset—pardon the pun."

Barrett arched a brow, trying not to smirk.

"You haven't answered my question," he said. "Are you going to look for a place?"

"Damn straight! Your cabin doesn't have electricity or plumbing. I need somewhere to run a hot tub after a long day of filming."

"Mm, hot tub," Barrett echoed. "I like the way you think."

"Then you'll help me pick a place out?" Lainey replied. "Something tells me you'll be spending a lot of time there, Officer Iron Feather…"

Impulsively, she kissed Barrett under the twinkling lights, only to feel him gently sway to the rhythm of the country music that started up again from the band on the grandstand.

"We made it, Lainey," Barrett whispered. "The film is finished, and your future couldn't be brighter."

He pressed his cheek against hers, relishing her soft, smooth skin, the heat of her body next to his, until a sharp ring burst from the mobile phone in his pocket. Barrett stopped their slow dance and sighed, pulling out his phone.

"Officer Iron Feather," he said, not even attempting to hide the irritation in his voice.

"Hey Barrett, this is Jean at dispatch. Are you still doing security for that movie they're filming near town?"

"As a matter of fact," Barrett replied, "the film just wrapped. This is my last night here. The cast and crew are currently at Memorial Park, if you want to come down for free ribs. They have champagne and everything."

"Ooh, I'll head over as soon as I get off work!" Jean said excitedly. "But the reason I'm calling is to give you a heads up. There's a guy headed your way who's hell bent on serving papers to one of the people employed by the Wings Channel. He and his lawyer stormed into the station just now demanding to know where the filming and crew was."

"Well, I'm afraid Easton Wolf is detained in the county jail, if that's who you're referring to. And the lead actor Cayden Hart may have already left town. So did a few crew members—"

"It's not for them—it's for a woman named Lainey Neil. Isn't she the star of the movie? The guy claimed he's her father and her manager, so she owes him twenty percent of all her earnings till she turns twenty-five. They said they have a legal summons ordering her to fork up back payments."

"What?" Barrett burst, fuming. "Can you repeat that?" He turned his cell phone on speaker so Lainey could hear.

"Gerald Neil is in town with his Hollywood lawyer, claiming his daughter owes him back pay as her manager from the time she was sixteen till the day she turns twenty-five."

"You gotta be kidding me!" Lainey yanked the phone from Barrett's hand. "That's impossible! My dad's been in prison on felony charges for real estate fraud up until last month."

Jean sighed. "It doesn't matter if he was in prison for a separate charge. They insist they have evidence that Lainey Neil never turned in a discontinuation of their contract. So despite his apparent prison term, he's *still* her manager."

"B-But Deb mailed that notice in for me!" Lainey cried. "When I was sixteen—she helped me do the paperwork and everything."

"Maybe it got lost in the mail?" Jean offered sympathetically.

At that moment, Lainey spied a slick red convertible hustling down Main Street, churning up a wake of dust. Who on earth drives a sports car on mountain dirt roads? she thought. Then the answer came to her.

Lawyers.

"Thanks for telling me, Jean," she said kindly, remembering her manners with a sigh before handing Barrett back his phone. Barrett ended the call and turned to stare at the sports car that was charging in a funnel of dirt down Main Street until it came to an abrupt halt beside Memorial Park.

"The devil has arrived," Lainey shook her head, "with an accomplice." She set her hands on her hips in disgust. "If you happen to feel like decking him again, Barrett, the way you did when we were fourteen, by all means, be my guest."

Barrett put away his phone and clenched his fists, as if he were thinking about it. "Of all the people to see right now, after you gave this film everything you had," he said. "Figures."

Rather than be a sitting duck, Lainey decided to beat her father to the punch by walking over to the convertible. "Dad!" she trilled with fake sweetness. So good to see you!"

The second her father climbed out of the passenger seat of the car, Lainey grabbed his shoulders and gave him a classic, Hollywood-style air kiss. "How lovely of you to visit me!" she enthused. "What's it been—eight whole years? Oh that's right, you were locked up for being a *criminal*."

Her father glared at her. Though he was decked out in a custom-tailored suit and designers shoes, probably purchased back when she was still his cash cow, he appeared far older than his fifty years after his time in prison. He took a drag on a black and gold cigarette and threw it to the ground, crushing it with his shoe.

"We aren't staying long, cupcake," Gerald told her gruffly. "This is my attorney, Ralph Woodcock, Esquire, and we're here to serve you papers."

Lainey narrowed her eyes. "*Don't* call me cupcake," she hissed. "And this is one hell of a greeting card, Dad—not that you've ever sent me any before," she pointed out. "If you think for one second I'm going to lay down and let you keep sucking the lifeblood out of my finances, you are wrong. I intend to fight you tooth and nail—"

"While you're back in prison," Barrett finished her sentence.

To Gerald's astonishment, Barrett showed him his badge. He whipped out his mobile phone and took a picture of Gerald's distinct tread mark in the dirt on Main Street. It was the same odd footprint with *Gucci* in the center that was beside the cabin door in Skystone Canyon. Then he slipped on gloves and picked up Gerald's cigarette butt, putting it into a ziplock bag. He removed his gloves and tucked them along with the bag into his pocket.

"You're under arrest," Barrett stated firmly.

"What? Who the hell is this jackass?" Gerald replied.

Barrett held up his fist. "You don't recognize these knuckles?" he said. "That's a shame, because they've gotten a whole lot more powerful than the fourteen-year old boy who decked you at horse camp ten years ago. Now, they're backed by the arm of the law. And legal evidence that proves you were at an arson crime scene this morning."

Barrett swiftly yanked the handcuffs from his pocket and proceeded to slap them onto Gerald's wrists, pinning him against the convertible.

"What the hell's going on!" Gerald yowled indignantly.

"Gerald Neil," Barret informed him, "you are under arrest for setting fire to the Skystone Canyon cabin, a historical building owned by the town of Bandits Hollow, and for deliberately sabotaging the successful completion of a film project by the Wings Channel. I suggest you drop all current charges against your daughter, as it only adds more evidence that you were in Bandits Hollow at the time of your crime. As head of security for this film project and a policeman for

Bandits Hollow, I am taking you to the Golden Wagon Hotel where another officer will transport you to the station. In the mean time, I will inform you of your rights."

"Holy shit! Arson, Gerry?" Robert Woodcock said, stunned as he backed away slowly from Lainey's father as if the man had contracted a communicable disease. "Seriously? And you expect anyone halfway sane to represent you?"

Robert headed over to the driver's side of the convertible and jumped in without bothering to open the door. Before Lainey's father could ask him what was going on, he'd already started up the engine. "You might as well call another lawyer while you're on your way to the station," he insisted, shaking his head. Then he threw the copy of the legal summons against Lainey into Gerald's face. "Because I'm outta here."

❧ 27 ❧

When Barrett returned after transferring Lainey's father to a police officer at the hotel, Lainey greeted him with a large plate of ribs, her fingers trembling a little. She handed the plate to him and stared at the ground. "I-I can't believe my dad even found me here, much less tried to burn down the cabin," she said, her voice still fragile. "Why would he do this?"

"He probably wanted you to be forced to take those jobs your agent was talking about so he'd make more money."

"But how would he even *know* about them?" she pressed. "It's not like my career offers are so glittering that they're talked about in the tabloids or something."

Lainey searched Barrett's eyes, watching him fall silent for a moment as he set down his plate of ribs on a nearby buffet table. When he returned, he ran his hands through her windswept hair.

"It's been a long day, Lainey, and you just received the shock of your life from your dad. As far as I'm concerned, the best cure is a slow dance with a lonesome cowboy who loves to look in your eyes. So why don't you tie your hair in a ribbon or something before we go kick off our shoes and dance barefoot in the grass of Memorial Park?" He piled her hair on top of her head, admiring her beautiful features. "You look stunning with your hair up."

"You're deliberately changing the subject, Officer Iron Feather."

"Am I?" he smiled, keeping his hands firmly on her hair. "See, it sets off your face." He gently stroked her temples.

"Maybe you're right," Lainey sighed. "Maybe I should just dance and enjoy the moment for a change at the barbeque. The film's finished. And my dad's gone, thank God—"

"And you could be in the arms of a man who's crazy about you," suggested Barrett. "I think it's time you stepped out of character and had a little fun."

Lainey blushed while her heart skipped a beat. "Has Ada Holdwell's seriousness rubbed off on me that much?" she asked, giving him a kiss on the cheek. "I kind of like your ribbon idea," she remarked, spotting Deb's makeup case next to the last remnants of film equipment by the parking area. She squeezed Barrett's hand and walked over to the case in order to fish around for hair ties, barrettes, bobby pins— whatever Deb might have on hand. When she opened the clasp, she found herself digging through piles of mascara, rouge and face powders, to no avail. Then she happened to notice there were several trays stacked on top of each another inside, so she carefully lifted them out until she reached the bottom. There, she didn't find hair ties or ribbons, but rather, a picture of a lovely teenage girl, smiling for what appeared to be a high school yearbook photo. Oddly enough, the girl looked a lot like Lainey at sixteen. When Lainey lifted up the photo, beneath it she discovered a small bag of poppers.

Just like the ones that had started the stampede—

Beside it was a vial labeled *Ipecac Syrup*, the kind of substance that could easily have simulated her so-called "food poisoning" after they'd gone to the bar.

Lainey sucked air, her heart pounding a mile a minute.

All at once, she felt a hand on her shoulder. She expected it to be Barrett, and she whipped around, ready to spill her findings.

But it was Deb.

"Why are there poppers in your makeup case?" Lainey asked, holding up the small bag. "Don't tell me gunpowder's good for pores?"

"I-I found them in the grass about a week ago, so I picked them up," Deb replied with her typical maternal smile. "I didn't want them to start a ruckus with the cows. But I guess I must have missed a few. I'm so sorry, Lainey."

"Then what about this bottle of ipecac?" she insisted. "A new method for making kin look dewy?" She shot a glance over at Barrett a couple of yards away, who tipped his hat at her. Something about the way he folded his arms told her everything...

He knew.

He'd probably known all along. But because Lainey was so close to Deb, he'd wanted her to find out herself.

Lainey felt a rush of blood flood her cheeks. Part of it was anger, naturally. But a much bigger part was the raw sting that someone she'd trusted as her closest confidant for the last eight years could have…

Betrayed her.

"Deb," Lainey corrected, "these poppers are fresh, straight out of the box. If they'd been left in the grass, like you said, the cigarette papers around them would have shriveled by now in the morning dew or afternoon rains."

"B-But I swear, Laura! You know I *always* want what's best for you. I've proven myself over and over—"

Lainey held up her hand to make her stop talking.

"Laura?" Lainey echoed, floored. "Did you just call me *Laura?*"

"She did. I heard it too," replied a low, husky voice. Lainey turned around, relieved to see Barrett had joined them.

"Oh, that's just my pet name for you on this film!" Deb backpedaled, smiling sweetly. "You know, Laura, from *Little House on the Prairie?* Like the way Harper always calls you pioneer girl. It's a term of endearment, honey."

Barrett gently grasped the photo of the teenage girl from Lainey's hand.

"It couldn't possibly have anything to do with Laura Griffin, who passed away ten years ago when she was sixteen years old, could it?"

Deb's eyes flared wide. Her mouth dropped open as if he'd slapped her.

Barrett reached out and clutched Lainey's hand for support. "It was a terrible auto accident, wasn't it? The way she was ripped from your heart—and your life—by a drunk driver in a matter of seconds. It was only natural for you to reach for the first person you could find to fill the void." He glanced at Lainey. "And even harder to allow the one who filled that hole in your heart to…grow up."

"I-I don't know what you're talking about," Deb fired back. "She's not gone. My daughter's perfectly fine! And she loves me. Don't you?" Deb thrust herself between Lainey and Barrett, giving Lainey a desperate hug. "You'll always love me —I'm your mother," she insisted, smoothing Lainey's hair. "Every sixteen-year-old girl needs her mother. She needs her ongoing guidance and support so she doesn't lose her way. Right, sweetie?"

Tears welled at the corners of Lainey's eyes. Shaking, she reached up and cupped Deb's cheeks. It was clear to her this woman still saw her as a lost teenager, needing to rely on a mother figure for direction. No wonder she'd done everything in her power to sabotage the *Skystone Canyon* film. For the first time in Lainey's career, she was playing a full-fledged adult— who fell in love, no less. Who demonstrated she was independent, and forged her own future.

"Of course," Lainey said kindly to Deb. "All girls need their mothers."

Lainey hugged her tightly, letting the tears roll down her cheeks. She rocked Deb in her arms for a moment, hoping that with her heart pressed against Deb's, she might somehow provide a measure of comfort for her soul. Finally, she wiped off her cheeks and made an effort to smile as she released her.

"Now that the movie has wrapped," Lainey said gently to Deb, "maybe it's time for a little break? Harper told me she's considering a…vacation…before production resumes on the *Skystone Canyon* series. She said there's an elegant retreat center in Colorado Springs. They specialize in treating overworked people who've might have, you know…issues…with addiction, anger, even loss and grief." Lainey snuck a glance at Barrett. "I hear the facility has a relaxing spa and a peaceful garden, as well as licensed, full-time counselors. And they schedule activities like art and yoga. I can come visit you, of course. What do you think?"

"I-I don't understand," replied Deb. "What is this place? How long do people stay there?"

"Usually about ninety days," Lainey said. "Sometimes longer…if they need to. Don't worry about the cost—it will be on me. Think of it as your own, state-of-the-art luxury escape, while you're between projects. And the best part is, you can call me every day."

"Um, that sounds nice, if you think it's a good idea, Laura," Deb replied in an unsettled tone.

"I do—I think it's a *very* good idea," insisted Lainey, stroking her cheek. "In fact, I'll give them a call tomorrow. We can start the online paperwork tonight. Okay?"

"You'll come visit me, Laura?"

"I will, as often as I can. I promise."

🦋 28 🐚

After Barret and Lainey drove Deb to the Serenity Ridge Treatment Center in Colorado Springs the following afternoon, they both remained present for her voluntary intake to the psychiatric wing of the facility, since Deb no longer had any close relatives who could vouch for her support. Though Deb seemed calm—and even happy—about the prospect of entering the facility by the time Barrett and Lainey had to leave, the experience left Lainey all choked up. She held back tears and hugged Deb with a tight grip before she was escorted away by a psychiatric technician. Lainey called out to her in a fragile voice, making Deb promise she'd phone with updates.

As soon as Barrett and Lainey stepped out into the parking lot, however, it was another story. Lainey clutched Barrett's hand fiercely as they headed to his Hummer. When they climbed inside, she burst into tears.

"She's the only mother I've ever had!" Lainey confessed, burying her face in her hands. "Ever since my mom died, I was basically the 'property' of my dad." She inhaled deeply to try and regulate her breaths. "That's why I can't bring myself to press charges. Deb obviously had problems I never knew about." Lainey turned to Barrett with tears sliding down her cheeks. "But she never *once* took money from me. For so long, she gave me love and support, Barrett, when nobody else did. I would have been a train wreck without her."

Barrett shifted in his seat, unsettled by Lainey's remarks as he started up the engine and pulled out of the parking lot. "I hear what you're saying," he noted in a tense tone. "But you do realize that Deb *purposely* never mailed that discontinuation of your management contract with your Dad, right? She may not have stolen money from you upfront, but as long as she could enable your dad to syphon off your funds, she could keep you small and dependent. In her mind, a sixteen-year-old girl who would need her forever."

Lainey nodded, knowing Barrett was telling the truth. And they both were certain now that Deb had been the one to sabotage her horse's saddle blanket and the wagon harness, along with engineering the food poisoning and the stampede. It had all been her twisted effort to keep a film featuring Lainey Neil as an adult from ever releasing. As the wind blew through Lainey's hair when they reached the highway that headed north to the mountains, Lainey wiped her eyes on her sleeve and turned to Barrett.

"Deb contacted my dad, didn't she?" Lainey said, her lips trembling. "She told him where I was and swiped a cabin key, knowing he'd try to bilk me for money again and would do anything to undermine the movie. She must've told him I could get more profitable roles, if I kept playing a washed-up child star in reality shows."

Lainey swallowed hard, her mind a swirl of realizations, unable to reconcile Deb's deviousness from her years of heartfelt support. "Barrett," Lainey asked, "do these behaviors make Deb…evil?"

Barrett laid his hand on her knee, remaining silent for a while as he navigated the curves through Ute Pass toward the mountains. He cleared his throat.

"Evil is something I've seen a lot of, Lainey," he replied. "I could tell you horror stories of murders and betrayals that I guarantee would keep you from sleeping at night. But Deb evil?" Barrett fell quiet again, mulling it over. "I'd say she's more like…desperate. And very, very confused."

Barrett shot Lainey a fiery glance that sent goosebumps charging down her spine. "But no matter how sad we think her story is, that doesn't mean Deb won't try to do it again. She's not firing on all cylinders, and she may never be okay."

"Do you think I should press charges?" Lainey asked. She clasped her hands, afraid of the answer.

Barrett rubbed her knee. "I think you should do what *you* need to make you feel you've done right by this person, who was a mother figure to you. So you can feel whole, Lainey. And my hunch is that the psychiatrists are going to keep her under observation at that facility for a very long time. But mark my word—if Deb's manipulations *ever* surface toward you again," Barrett met her gaze with a burning protectiveness, "I'm throwing her ass in jail."

~

B y the time Barrett and Lainey reached Bandits Hollow, darkness had begun to seep over the town, and the Victorian streetlamps glowed over the boardwalks. Lainey glanced up from the Hummer, spying a couple of stars that had already come out and begun to twinkle. The cool air rifling through her hair felt refreshing, and she was glad to be out of the city and in a quieter, more remote setting. But when Barrett pulled the Hummer up to the Golden Wagon Hotel, Lainey became a bit puzzled.

"Don't tell me you're dropping me off here tonight," she said nervously. "I realize I have one more night paid for by the Wings Channel, but I'm not sure I can handle, you know… your ancestor…right now."

At that moment, the insistent call of an owl echoed across Main Street, making Lainey jump.

Barrett smirked a little. He glanced at the silhouette of a great horned owl perched on top of a lamppost and nodded. "Nope," he said resolutely, "I think somebody has other plans for us tonight."

"Plans? What do you mean?" asked Lainey.

Barrett smiled and got out of the Hummer, walking around to open her door.

"Come with me and find out," he urged, taking her by the hand. They walked up to the hotel and Barrett swung open the mahogany front door. Then he led her across the plush lobby to a meeting room on the left side of the grand staircase. When he opened the door, to Lainey's astonishment, there were hundreds of people seated in the darkened room, watching the final scene from *Skystone Canyon*. Lainey spied Lander and Dillon in the back row, eating popcorn, while her face appeared on the screen, larger than life, telling Barrett that the sky was big enough for both of them. As the two characters kissed, everyone in the room began to cheer. The camera lens pulled back to reveal two lovers in an embrace beside a cabin in Skystone Canyon, with the majestic Rocky Mountain towering over them in the background, and then the film stopped. Harper Stone stepped in front of the screen.

"Well, Bandits Hollow, you haven't gotten rid of us yet!" she chided the audience. "I'd like to thank the entire town for allowing our crew to film here. We'll be seeing you to film the new, streaming TV series in a couple of months."

A round of applause rippled through the crowd, and Lainey was puzzled when Barrett began walking with her toward the screen as soft, elegant music started to play from the room's speakers. Harper's face became more serious for a moment.

"As you know, the film *Skystone Canyon* is a love story," she told the audience, "and life has a funny way of imitating art. During our experience here, we've had our share of mishaps—a stampede, food poisoning, a cabin burning. And then there were the people who quit—or got arrested, thank God."

The audience laughed at the truthful bite in her words.

"But just like Ada Holdwell and Nate Proctor in the film, we prevailed. And best of all, we proved that love still survives."

At that moment, handwritten words appeared on the screen on lined binder paper, the kind typically used in high school.

"And what I want the good people of Bandits Hollow to know is that it's been a privilege to watch love do more than survive. We've actually been honored to see it grow."

Lainey shook her head, wondering what Harper was talking about as she stepped away from the screen. Oddly, Barrett tugged Lainey's hand and led her to the center of the front of the room, where he began to read the words on the screen aloud.

Dear Lainey,

I think about you every day. I imagine your sweet face and sparkling blue eyes. It was the hardest thing in the world for me to watch you go. But one day, I promise with all my heart, if I ever get the chance to see you again, I'm going to ask you to marry me.

Lainey noticed the date on the screen was exactly ten years ago, right after she'd left horse camp. The next image that surfaced on the screen showed two stacks of letters, each over a foot high. In the following frame, the camera roamed over the postmarks of the letters that were spread out on a table. All of the postmarks were from Bandits Hollow over the last decade, and each letter was addressed to Lainey Neil from Barrett Iron Feather.

Lainey's breath hitched. Barrett *had* been writing to her—for ten solid years!

"Barrett," she gasped, searching his face, "where on earth did you find these?"

Barrett gazed into her eyes. "When we were helping Deb pack this morning to go to her new facility today. She dropped one of her suitcases and it tumbled open. It was full of these letters—along with your post office box key," He smiled lovingly at Lainey. "I told her I'd hang on to them for safekeeping."

Lainey's eyes misted, her mind reeling. So Deb had confiscated Barrett's letters all these years. She'd trusted Deb to get her mail at the post office ever since she was a teen, having no idea she was swiping the letters...

In the next frame on the screen, however, there appeared a final letter, handwritten with the current day's date.

"Miss Lainey Neil," Barrett said, "I would like the honor of delivering this last letter to you personally." He handed her an envelope. "Would you mind reading it aloud?"

Heart pounding, Lainey opened it and scanned the handwriting—Barrett's handwriting—the same words that appeared on the screen.

"Go ahead!" Harper urged from the side of the screen. "Read the letter aloud!"

Dear Lainey,

From the time we were fourteen, I knew you were the one for me. There's never been anyone else I could imagine spending my life with who comes close to you. I promise to love you with all my heart and to protect and cherish you for the rest of your days.

To her surprise, Barrett dropped to one knee and held out a ring box to Lainey.

"Will you marry me, Lainey Neil?" he asked.

Hands trembling, Lainey grasped the box and slowly opened it. Inside was a beautiful diamond ring flanked by two turquoise stones of pure, exquisite blue.

Sky stones…

Lainey picked up the ring. All at once, she could have
sworn she heard Barrett's ancestor singing again—the same
song she'd heard in the hotel. It was soft, barely above a
whisper, almost as though it were emanating from inside the
ring's stones. Startled, she glanced around the room, curious if
anyone else could hear the song. The audience merely gazed at
her with rapt attention, waiting on her response to Barrett. It
was then Lainey recalled Iron Feather's mysterious words.

*Remember shich'choonii, listen to him—to his love. And to the sky
stones.*

Lainey glanced into Barrett's brown eyes, as full of hope as
his character in *Skystone Canyon*. He studied the turquoise stones
on the ring and then met her gaze with an intrigued look, as
though he could hear the song, too. Two hearts, laced together
by the same notes. Lainey smiled and tugged on his arm to
stand up, and she leaned her forehead against his. Then she
slipped the ring on her finger, showing off for the crowd to
their applause. Before Barrett could blink, Lainey snuck the
handcuffs from his pocket and slapped them on his wrist
and hers.

"Looks like you're stuck with me now, Officer Iron
Feather," she teased.

"Is that a yes?" Barrett smirked.

"Yes!" replied Lainey.

Barrett grinned and held up their locked hands to the
crowd. "Good thing I believe in happy endings. And in the sky
stones' song," he whispered, giving her a kiss.

In that moment, Lainey spied a great horned owl through
the window that had silently landed on a tree branch outside

the room, its feathers illuminated by the light of the movie screen. But this time, she didn't tremble or even flinch at the odd omen. She simply nudged Barrett until he saw it, too. Then she gave the bird a wink and whispered, "Thank you— we'll be listening," before she circled her arms around Barrett's neck. With a big smile, Barrett dove into Lainey's lips for a long and dreamy kiss.

JICARILLA APACHE LANGUAGE GLOSSARY

The fictional characters in *Skystone Canyon* are neither full-blood Apache nor fluent speakers of the Jicarilla Apache language. In the story, however, Barrett Iron Feather acquired a few words in childhood from his mother who grew up on the Jicarilla Apache Reservation. The following Jicarilla Apache words featured in the novel are listed in alphabetical order with translations and approximate phonetic pronunciations in English. Please bear in mind that many Apache sounds do not exist in English, and Apache is a tonal language with rises, falls, nasalizations, glottal stops, and various tongue aspirations that indicate different word nuances. As a result, pronunciation accuracy can only be given justice by listening to a native Apache speaker. All Jicarilla Apache terms in *Skystone Canyon* were derived from either native speakers or the source most trusted by the Jicarilla Apache Nation: *Dictionary of Jicarilla Apache* by Wilhelmina Phone, Maureen Olson, and Matilda

Martinez published by the University of New Mexico Press, 2007. Generous assistance was also provided by Vernon Petago, Heritage Specialist at the Jicarilla Apache Cultural Affairs Office in Dulce, New Mexico.

dáatł'iiji: (dahkl + ee + jih) **turquoise.** The accent mark indicates a long vowel sound with a falling tone, and the apostrophe indicates a brief stop. The double vowels without accents indicate long vowel sounds. The "tł" consonant has a lateral tongue aspiration, which is like adding an airy "k" sound before the "l", starting from a "d" tongue position.

gaałkiił: (gahkl + ee + kl) **storm.** The double vowels indicate long vowel sounds, and the underlined double vowels include a nasalized tone. The "ł" consonant has a lateral tongue aspiration, which is like adding an airy "k" sound before the "l".

ha'dish'aí: (ha + desh + ai) **I am singing.** Apostrophes indicate brief stops, and the accent over the last vowel indicates it is pronounced with a high tone.

hayiiłka: (hah + yeekl + kah) **sunrise.** The double vowels indicate long vowel sounds, and the "ł" consonant has a lateral tongue aspiration, which is like adding an airy "k" sound before the "l".

jígonaa'áí: (jeh +goanah + ai) **the sun.** The accent over the vowels indicate they are pronounced with a high tone, and the double vowels indicate long vowel sounds. The apostrophes indicate a brief stop.

saayi: (sah + yeh) **sand.** The double vowels indicate long vowel sounds.

shich'oonii: (shich + oan + ee) **my friend.** The apostrophe indicates a brief stop.

ADDITIONAL TERMS

Apache: (ah + pach + ee) A Spanish word referring to the southern Athabaskan-speaking native people residing in the American Southwest and northern Mexico. To differentiate among groups, the Spanish explorers added various suffixes, such as "Apache de Jicarilla" to identify the particular band that resided in northern New Mexico and southern Colorado. Though the origin of the word Apache in Spanish is uncertain, it may be based upon the Zuni term *'a paču*, meaning "enemies". Today, the Jicarilla Apache still use the term Apache to refer to their nation as well as the word *Dinde* (din + deh) or *Tinde* (tin + deh), meaning "The People", to refer to themselves in their own language.

Jicarilla: (hick + ah + ree + ya) Spanish word for "little basket, gourd, or cup" as well as for "little basket maker." The Spanish employed the term "Jicarilla" to describe the Apache band near Rio Chama in northern New Mexico and southern Colorado due to their extraordinary craftsmanship in weaving baskets. In addition to their artistic skills, the Spanish later learned that the Jicarilla Apache were also notoriously effective warriors.

ABOUT THE AUTHOR

USA TODAY bestselling author Diane J. Reed writes happily ever afters with a touch of magic that make you believe in the power of love. Her stories feed the soul with outlaws, mavericks, and dreamers who have big hearts under big skies and dare to risk all for those they cherish. Because love is more than a feeling—it's the magic that changes everything.

To get the latest on new releases, sign up for Diane J. Reed's newsletter at dianejreed.com.

Made in the USA
Middletown, DE
26 August 2018